The Kids Left.
The Dog Died. Now What?

Book, Music and Lyrics by
Carole Caplan-Lonner

Music Consultant
Rick Hip-Flores

A SAMUEL FRENCH ACTING EDITION

SAMUEL
FRENCH
FOUNDED 1830

NEW YORK HOLLYWOOD LONDON TORONTO

SAMUELFRENCH.COM

ISBN 978-0-573-69833-0   Printed in U.S.A.   #29638

RENTAL MATERIALS

An orchestration consisting of a **Piano/Vocal** Score will be loaned two months prior to the production ONLY on the receipt of the Licensing Fee quoted for all performances, the rental fee and a refundable deposit.

Please contact Samuel French for perusal of the music materials as well as a performance license application.

IMPORTANT BILLING AND CREDIT
REQUIREMENTS

All producers of *THE KIDS LEFT. THE DOG DIED. NOW WHAT?* *must* give credit to the Author of the Play in all programs distributed in connection with performances of the Play, and in all instances in which the title of the Play appears for the purposes of advertising, publicizing or otherwise exploiting the Play and/or a production. The name of the Author *must* appear on a separate line on which no other name appears, immediately following the title and *must* appear in size of type not less than fifty percent of the size of the title type.

Society Hill Playhouse

507 South 8th Street
50th Anniversary Season
Jay & Deen Kogan: Founding Directors

The Kids Left.
The Dog Died.
Now What?

A New Musical
By
Carole Caplan-Lonner

With

Corbin Abernathy · Amy Walton

Gerri Weagraff · Paul Weagraff

Director	Musical Director	Choreographer
T.J. Sokso	Zach Wiseley	Samuel Reyes

Scenic Design	Lighting Design	Costume Design	Visual Designs
Jacob Walton	Rick Belzer	Lauren Perigard	Amanda Nesco

Stage Manager	Production Coordinator	Press Representative
Bayla Rubin	G DeCandia	Carole Morganti

Musical Consultant
Rick Hip-Flores

The Kids Left. The Dog Died. Now What? was first produced as part of
the New York Musical Theatre Festival, September 2007

Society Hill Playhouse proudly participates in the Barrymore Awards for
Excellence in Theatre, a program of the Theatre Alliance of Greater Philadelphia.

CHARACTERS

WOMAN – 50ish

WOMAN – 40-45

2 MEN – 50 to 55ish

The cast is comprised of four actors, who play numerous roles using props & costume pieces. Community theaters have the option of using 4-36 different actors if they wish:

4 actors: Divide up all characters; original form

6 actors: (4 original plus 2) **EMILY, MICHAEL** – all other characters divided

8 actors: (4 original plus 4) **EMILY, MICHAEL, MARVIN, WIDOW** – all other roles divided

9-36 actors: (4 orginal plus...) **EMILY, MICHAEL, MARVIN, WIDOW, MISTRESS** – the rest divided

SETTING

One baby grand piano (two is even better!). Backdrop is a large framed empty screen. Photos change with each scene indicating setting.

AUTHOR'S NOTES

I was brought up in the golden age of musicals. I watched Eliza and Adelaide and Anna and was fascinated by the problems they faced and the times in which they lived. It was all so wonderful. I was forever stage struck. But as I grew older, it seemed to me that no one was writing a musical about my life, my problems, and my times.

So when the kids left and the dog died, I decided I would write a musical I wanted to see! I started analyzing my group of empty-nester friends. How were they coping with what life threw at them? What were they really thinking as they went about their daily lives? And how were they unique from past generations? I soon realized that basically people have always been the same, but it's the time in which they live that makes them unique. So I set out to tell our story.

Back to my friends I went seeking inspiration. I wondered why some seemed to rise to life's challenges while others simply succumbed. It didn't take long to discover the answer: humor. Looking back I realized my grandparents and parents had used humor to cope with immigration, the Great Depression and wars. Humor makes it possible for us to exist...thus, *THE KIDS LEFT. THE DOG DIED. NOW WHAT?* was created.

A twenty-year journey followed. This musical has had five different titles, three readings, four staged workshops, and a successful, sold-out run in the 2007 New York Musical Festival. This led to a full production at Philadelphia's 'Society Hill Playhouse' in 2009 and to my great satisfaction that a musical has arrived that reflects my time and maybe yours.

Carole Caplan-Lonner

ACKNOWLEDGEMENTS

Special thanks to Bernie Katz, Edie Broida, Jeff Sweet, Peter Filichia, Peter Franklin and Harold Prince for believing in me and in helping my fantasy become a reality.

SCENES & SONGS

Scene One: New Beginnings
Full Company:
Song 1: "Now What?"
Voice Over: Answering Machine Message-3

Scene Two: Technology
Ben & Alice
Song 2: "Who Says Progress Is Good?"

Scene Three: Meet Marvin # 1
Marvin
Song 3: "Doctors"
Voice Over: Answering Machine Message-1

Scene Four: Never Alone
Emily
Song 4: "Firsts"

Scene Five: The Visit
Grandparents: Barbara, Chuck, Jan, Larry
Song 5: "Headlights / Tail Lights"

Scene Six: The Happy Couple
Bob & Judy
Song 6: "If You Want To Stay Married"
Voice Over: Answering Machine Message-2

Scene Seven: Armani
Emily, Pam

Scene Eight: Doctors Reprise #2
Marvin
Song 7: "Doctors" (Reprise 1)

Scene Nine: Cheap Spot
Dave, Sara, Fred & Karin
Song 8: "Everyone's Got A Cheap Spot"

Scene Ten: Computer #1
Emily, Girlfriend Michael & Friend.

Scene Eleven: Stuck In The Middle
Joey
Song 9: "Sandwich Generation"

Scene Twelve: Wedding Reception
Peter /Elaine (plus Dance Partners)
Song 10: "It's not a Date"

Scene Thirteen: Time Moves On
All
Song 11: "Now What?" (Reprise)

Scene Fourteen: Doctors
Marvin
Song 12: "Doctors" (Reprise 2)

Scene Fifteen: It's Not My Fault
Insurance Adjuster & Client
Song 13: "I Got A Case"

Scene Sixteen: Computer #2
Emily & Michael
Song 14: "The Chat"
Voice Over: Answering Machine Message

Scene Seventeen: Thursday Meet Widow
Mistress Meets Widow

Scene Eighteen: Temptation
Ted & Melinda
Song 15: "Perfect Bliss"

Scene Nineteen: Aarp
Ralph (Plus Greek Chorus Of Three)
Song 16: "AARP"

Scene Twenty: He's Got To Eat
Liz. Peggy, Susie (Man Dressed As Woman)
Song 17:"Casserole Stroll"
Voice Over: Answering Machine Message

Scene Twenty-One: Here Comes Marvin #4
Marvin

Scene Twenty-Two One Ball Game
Michael & Emily
Song 18: "New Firsts" (Reprise)

Scene Twenty-Three: Finale
Full Company:
Song 19: "Now What" (Reprise)

This play is dedicated to my mother Sylvia, my daughters Nancy and Jane, and to all of my delightful grandchildren who have showed me the joys of an empty nest.

ACT ONE

(FRAMED BACKGROUND PHOTO: The frame contains the empty nest logo.)

(The piano is playing "Rock-a-bye-baby." An explosion sound effect buttons the song. **WOMAN ONE** *appears transfixed in a pool of light. Each actor enters on their own verse, singing with a tone of crisis.)*

Scene One: Now What?

SONG: (1) "NOW WHAT?"

WOMAN TWO. *(with the bewilderment of a six year-old)*
YOU WAKE ONE MORNING
YOU'RE SIX YEARS OLD
YOU KISS YOUR MOTHER
DO AS YOUR TOLD
YOUR LIFE'S ADVENTURES
WILL SOON UNFOLD
AND YOU'RE ALWAYS THINKING – NOW WHAT?

*(***MAN ONE*** enters.)*

MAN ONE.
IT'S TEN YEARS LATER
YOU'RE AT A DANCE
THE GIRLS ARE PRETTY
YOU TAKE A CHANCE
YOU THINK YOU'RE SEXY-
IN LEATHER PANTS
AND STILL YOU'RE WONDERING – NOW WHAT?

*(***WOMAN ONE*** enters.)*

WOMAN ONE.

> TIME MOVES ON AND IT LEAVES YOU INSECURE
> 'CAUSE WITH NO GUARANTEES YOU FIND
> NOTHING IS FOR SURE
> THINGS ARE FINE,
> THEN YOU'RE FORCED TO MAKE A CHANGE

> (**MAN TWO** *enters.*)

ALL.

> AND EVERY THING NEW FEELS SO HORRIBLY STRANGE

MAN TWO.

> YOU'RE OFF TO COLLEGE
> YOU DRINK A LOT.
> THE BOOKS YOU STUDIED
> ARE SOON FORGOT
> THE ROAD IS EASY
> OR SO YOU THOUGHT

ALL.

> AND YOU GOT A LUMP IN YOUR GUT!
> NOW WHAT?

> (*dialogue break with music underscore:*)

WOMAN ONE (AS EMILY). When you get to my age it's always something. Just when you think you've got life mastered, oops, another challenge And, as I've come to realize, I'm not the only one who experiences these periodic jolts. There are millions of people just like you and me. Tonight we will be presenting a musical revue –

MAN ONE. Oh, not another revue!

EMILY. Well, maybe there'll be a little story in there somewhere.

MAN ONE. Promise?

EMILY. In fact, you'll witness the stories of, oh say, thirty of us.

WOMAN TWO. I have indigestion from all the words I've eaten.

MAN TWO. Apparently a steady diet of potato chips does not lead to optimal health.

WOMAN TWO. All these gadgets make me feel stupid.

MAN ONE. I'm not cheap. It's just that one little expense that bugs me.

MAN TWO. My mom is 92, my daughter is 18, and they're both driving me nuts!

WOMAN ONE. Okay, okay. Don't give it all away just yet. Remember, everything in due course-one stage at a time.

WOMAN TWO.

    YOU PLAN THE WEDDING

MAN ONE.

    YOU GET YOUR RAISE

WOMAN TWO.

    YOU HAVE A MORTGAGE

MAN TWO.

    YOU'RE IN A DAZE

ALL.

    YOU'RE ALWAYS THINKING
    IT'S JUST A PHASE
    AND YOU'RE LEFT THERE GUESSING – NOW WHAT?

    THE BABY'S CRYING
    YOU GET NO SLEEP
    THE BILLS ARE PILING
    'CAUSE NOTHING'S CHEAP
    YOU KEEP ON TRYING
    YOU'RE IN THIS DEEP
    AND YOU'RE ALWAYS THINKING-NOW WHAT?

    TIME MOVES ON AND IT MAKES YOU INSECURE
    'CAUSE WITH NO GUARANTEES
    YOU FIND NOTHING IS FOR SURE
    THINGS ARE FINE,
    THEN YOU'RE FORCED TO MAKE A CHANGE
    AND EVERY THING NEW FEELS SO HORRIBLY STRANGE

    THE HOUSE IS EMPTY
    THE KIDS ARE GONE
    THE DOG IS BURIED
    NEED I GO ON

ALL. *(cont.)*
> YOU'RE BORED AND RESTLESS
> YOU MOW THE LAWN
> AND THE HOUSE IS SUDDENLY BIGGER
> AND THE NEIGHBORS MOVIN' AWAY
> AND THE KIDS HAVE SUDDENLY VANISHED
> AND YOUR MOTHER'S COMING TO STAY
> AND THEY SAY IT'S TIME TO RETIRE
> BUT IT SEEMS LIKE SUCH A CLICHE
> AND YOU GOT A LUMP IN YOUR GUT
> NOW WHAT?

VOICE OVER: ANSWERING MACHINE. *(rewind sound)*

MACHINE VOICE. You have three messages.

> *(beep)*

DAUGHTER. Hi Dad, I'm at the airport. Where ARE you!? *(whispers to a friend next to him:)* He's not there. *(continues into phone)* Dad, I just realized I forgot my computer. It was really stupid of me. If you get this message in the next 20 minutes you'll still have time to run it out. If you don't, PLEASE Fed Ex it immediately. *(to her friend:)* He's gonna kill me!

> *(beep)*

GRANDMOTHER. Hello my dear, this is your mother calling. In case you're wondering where your car is – I've taken it. I'm at Costco buying you a new toaster; never liked yours. They're on sale so I'm buying you two. You can never tell when one might break.

> *(beep)*

GRANDSON. Hi Grandma. Mommy said I can't have a dog. I want one. You said I could have whatever I wanted for my birthday. Can we go tomorrow?

> *(beep)*

Scene Two: Technology

(FRAMED BACKGROUND PHOTO: A living room. On stage are two chairs and a coffee table. **WOMAN TWO [ALICE]** *enters exhausted. She throws her coat down and plops in a chair.)*

ALICE. *(calling to husband offstage)* Hi Honey, I'm home.

*(***MAN ONE*** enters as ***BEN*** with a gift behind his back.)*

BEN. You look exhausted.

ALICE. Try six hours with a four year-old and no TV.

BEN. What do you mean, no TV?

ALICE. Our kids got one of those new TV systems with umpteen remotes and I couldn't figure out how to turn the damn thing on. There's something wrong with our society when you can't turn on a television set in someone else's house!

BEN. Cheer up Alice. I bought you a present.

ALICE. Really?

(He gives her a gift box, tied in a ribbon.)

BEN. You're going to love it!

ALICE. Oh good. I love presents!

(She takes the ribbon off the box and looks inside. She looks very disappointed.)

What's this?

BEN. It's the new IQ180. They say it's the latest in technology.

ALICE. *(Annoyed, she pulls it out and holds it up as though it was a piece of rotten fish.)* This is not a present. I've told you it's not a present if it comes with a plug. You're just wasting our money?

BEN. It's progress. We got to stay in touch with technology! You saw the look we got from the kids when we vetoed the new TiVo. Besides, listen to this…

(He reads from the pamphlet.)

BEN. *(cont.)* The new IQ180 comes loaded with the following apps: ESPN Sports updates, it's even got a Star Wars light saber. *(demonstrates with sound effect)* It's got a song finder. *(sings)* And in a pinch it can even be used as a shaver. *(demonstrates with sound effect)*

ALICE. Another gadget – another excuse to waste time.

BEN. And get this – *(seductively)* you can adjust the lighting levels of any room in your house.

(He throws the directions over his shoulder and continues to come on to **ALICE.***)*

You always complain certain lighting is very unflattering. Here's your chance.

ALICE. *(avoiding his advances)* Who cares?

BEN. Just try it.

ALICE. No, I don't want to. All your gadgets make me feel – stupid.

BEN. You just have to have a little patience. Try it.

ALICE. *(giving in)* Okay, so what do I push?

BEN. The button on the left.

(She pushes a button. Nothing happens.)

ALICE. Nothing's happening.

BEN. *(He looks.)* Push it again.

(He shows her. She tries pushing a few more times. All the lights go out.)

BEN. Oh shit. It looked so easy at the store.

ALICE. This is not a present! Jewelry is a present!!!

BEN. Now just relax.

ALICE. I can't see a damn thing. Thanks to you, Mr. Technology.

(They stumble around in the dark, bumping furniture.)

BEN. I'll get the directions.

ALICE. What good are directions if you can't see? Some progress!

BEN. Wait, I got this mini flashlight on my keychain.

ALICE. Do me a favor and see if they have a tech support number.

(He proceeds to read directions with his mini light.)

BEN. Oh, here we go. Look it says, "To operate instrument go to the menu wheel. Select Option B. Turn the jog dial."

ALICE. *(flustered)* Oh, give me the directions. This is not for us. If they wanted people our age to use this stuff they would have made the print bigger.

(She holds the directions at arm's length and tries reading them again.)

BEN. Okay, see if they have a tech support number?

(Music intro starts.)

ALICE. Okay I got it.

BEN. Give me the gizmo.

(He takes the device. She dials the land phone.)

ALICE. Hold the light so I can see.1-800-72 *(continues to dial)* …we need this like a hole in the head.

(He takes the IQ180 phone. We hear him grumbling. Eventually all the lights go on.)

What did you push?

BEN. I'm not sure. Stay on the line with tech support.

*(He crosses away from **ALICE** and sits down)*

SONG: (2) "WHO SAYS PROGRESS IS GOOD?"

(Song sung at a fast clip.)

SO MANY GADGETS!
SO MUCH TO LEARN!
SO MANY TOYS YOU BOUGHT I WISH WE COULD RETURN
WHAT HAPPENED TO THE WORLD I UNDERSTOOD?
TELL ME WHO SAYS PROGRESS IS GOOD?

BEN. Think of how impressed the kids will be when they see you using it.

ALICE. How do you even turn it on?

BEN. That's simple. You push the button and hold for five seconds, slide to unlock, enter your code...

ALICE.

> IT'S SUCH A HASSLE!
> IT'S SUCH A WASTE!
> ANOTHER MARVELOUS DEVICE TO GET MISPLACED!
> IS THIS THE WAY TO SPEND ONE'S LIVELIHOOD?
> I'D SAY "HOORAY FOR PROGRESS"
> BUT WHO SAYS PROGRESS IS GOOD?"

BEN. Now just look here. You select the icon you want to use – camera, address book, iPod – it's not that complicated.

ALICE.

> I REMEMBER WHEN LIFE WAS SIMPLER.
> WHEN I COULD OPERATE APPLIANCES WITH EASE.
> BUT NOW MY HOURS ARE FILLED READING DIRECTIONS
> AND GETTING TECH SUPPORT FROM OVERSEAS.

TECH SUPPORT V.O. *(with Eastern Indian accent)* Your call will be answered in the order it was received. Your estimated wait time is now seven to twenty–three minutes.

ALICE.

> I'M SICK OF HOLDING!
> THIS IS ABSURD!
> WHAT'S EVEN WORSE IS I WON'T UNDERSTAND A WORD.
> I'D TAKE A HAMMER TO IT IF I COULD.
> CAUSE EVERY DAY ITS PROGRESS,
> BUT WHO SAYS PROGRESS IS GOOD?

BEN. It says here, you can fit 3000 of your favorite songs... in this little gadget!

ALICE. I don't have 3000 favorite songs!

> WHATEVER HAPPENED TO CONVERSATION,
> OR A VACATION-THE TWO OF US ALONE?
> THOSE QUIET MOMENTS HAVE NOW BEEN INTERRUPTED
> WITH, "DID YOU SEE MY FAX?"AND "WHERE'S MY PHONE?"

BEN. Hey, look at this. You'll never get lost with the GPS system. It even has a key chair attachment that will always lead you to your car when you're lost in the parking lot... AND it gives immediate sale alerts at all the local department stores.

(Music changes mood.)

ALICE. Really?

(Hesitantly she trades her land phone for the IQ180.)

MAYBE THIS ONE TIME
I'LL TAKE A CHANCE.
JUST FOR THIS ONE EXTENUATING CIRCUMSTANCE.
IF I CAN HIT THE SALES AT BLOOMINGDALES
AND THEN FIND MY CAR AT THE MALL
HEY MAYBE ALL THIS PROGRESS,
IS PROGRESS, AFTER ALL!

Does it come in pink?

Scene Three: Meet Marvin

(FRAMED BACKGROUND PHOTO: Blank. **MAN TWO [MARVIN]** *enters wearing a casual sporty outfit. He wears this outfit each time he appears as* **MARVIN**.*)*

MARVIN. *(startled momentarily by the audience)* Oh, hey, how ya doing? You know, I've figured out there are two types of people in this world: those who have bad backs and those that will. If God had expected me to stand up on my own two feet for fifty-eight years I wish he had taken a few extra minutes when he was designing backs. Fortunately I've got Dr. Bernstein, my spine specialist. He got my back working so I can play golf again,

(He practices his swing and then his knee goes out. He holds his knee and hops on his other leg back across the stage.)

But then my knee went out and that led to Dr. Brown-best knee man in *[Name city you're in].* My game is really improving, but I think it's partly because Dr. Atwater, my psychologist, gave me a valuable suggestion. He said, "If you want your game to improve, you have to get your priorities straight and be prepared to make sacrifices." So...I'm seeing a lot less of my family.

*(***MARVIN*** sings:)*

SONG: (3) "DOCTORS"

IF YOU HURT YOUR FOOT
IF YOU TURN YOUR WRIST
IF THAT NASTY STOMACH FLU CONTINUES TO PERSIST
IF YOU'VE LOST YOUR PEP

(puts his hands over his privates)

AND YOU'RE IN A STEW
WHO DO YOU CALL?
DOCTORS – THAT'S WHO

Now that I've put golf before my family, I'm shooting even par. Maybe if I get divorced I can make the senior tour.

(Enter **MAN ONE, WOMAN ONE,** *and* **WOMAN TWO,**
wearing white lab-coats. **MAN ONE** *helps* **MARVIN** *into a*
hospital gown as he sings.)

MARVIN. *(cont.)*

IF YOU'RE PLAYING GOLF
AND YOU TWIST YOUR NECK
NOW YOU CAN'T GET OFF YOUR BUTT
YOU'RE THINKING "WHAT THE HECK"
IF YOU BURN YOUR HAND

*(***MAN ONE** *examines his hand and sprays it with disin-*
fectant taken from his pocket.)

ON THE BARBECUE
THEN, WHO DO YOU CALL?
DOCTORS – THAT'S WHO

*(***MAN ONE** *exits.* **WOMAN ONE** *with a stethoscope, blood*
pressure gadget, and a tongue depressor goes to work on
MARVIN*. She takes his pulse, etc. while he sings.)*

YOU DON'T CALL YOUR CONGRESSMAN
YOUR GROCERY CLERK
YOUR LAWYA
THEY GOT NOTHING FOR YA
ONLY PHONY AIRS

YOU DON'T CALL YOUR DRINKING PALS
THE OFFICE GALS
WON'T SAVE YA
JUST GIVE ME A LITTLE WHITE COAT AND A STETHOSCOPE
AND I KNOW THAT SOMEONE CARES

*(***WOMAN ONE** *exits.* **WOMAN TWO** *unhooks the back*
of **MARVIN** *'s gown. While he sings she pulls a purple*
rubber glove from her pocket.)

WHEN YOUR COLON'S BLOCKED
AND YOU'RE LOOKING GREEN
WHEN YOUR STOMACH'S ON THE FRITZ
AND YOU THINK IT'S YOUR SPLEEN
IF YOUR FINGER'S STUCK
ON THE CRAZY GLUE

(**WOMAN TWO** *checks his prostate from behind.*)

MARVIN. *(cont.)*

WHO DO YOU CALL?
I'LL GIVE YOU A CLUUUUE!

(reacting from glove insertion)

YOU CALL YOUR ALLERGIST
UROLOGIST,
YOUR TRUSTY PHARMACOLOGIST,
AND YOU'LL FEEL SUBLIME
CAUSE DOCTORS HAVE THE ANSWERS EVERY TIME.

ANSWERING MACHINE VOICE OVER. *(beep)* Hi, Emily. It's just me calling to remind you that Ed and I will come by to pick you up at seven, and this time no excuses-okay?! Just remember we're all your good friends. We love you and you've got to get out. Trust me you're going to have a good time.

(beep)

Scene Four: Never Alone

(FRAMED BACKGROUND PHOTO: Master bedroom. Stage setting consists of a full length, mirror-less frame, a coat stand, and small table with framed photo. **WOMAN ONE [EMILY]** *is getting ready for a night out. She puts on a necklace then, unsure of herself, tries on a second necklace. She looks thru the mirror frame and talks to her reflection.)*

EMILY. You're going to have a good time. You're going to have a good time!

(pause)

SONG: (4) "FIRSTS"

*(***EMILY*** *puts on her lipstick. A belt and then goes to a small table where she starts to load her purse. She glances at a photo of her late husband, Roger.)*

EMILY. Roger, Roger...Roger...

(She sings.)

I WAS YOUR FIRST LOVE,
AND YOU MY FIRST BEAU.
THEY THOUGHT US TOO YOUNG THEN
BUT IT WASN'T SO.
I THINK OF OUR WEDDING,
OUR HONEYMOON,
WE SPENT OUR FIRST NIGHT,
SOFT CRIES OF DELIGHT,
FIRST BABY CAME SOON.

SO MANY FIRSTS WE GOT TO SHARE
THERE NEVER WAS EVER A HAPPIER PAIR.
FIRST JOB PROMOTION,
WE BOTH WORKED SO HARD
FIRST SECONDHAND CHEVY,
FIRST HOME WITH A YARD.

OFFSTAGE VOICE. Emily, we're downstairs. Are you ready?

EMILY. I'll be there in a minute.

NOW THERE ARE NEW FIRSTS
SETTING THE TONE.
FIRST DOVER SOLE DINNER
I'M EATING ALONE.
THE FIRST TIME I'M SLEEPING
ALONE IN OUR BED.
THE FIRST MEAL I COOK,
THE FIRST TRIP THAT I BOOK,
FOR JUST ONE INSTEAD.
SO MANY FIRSTS
COME INTO VIEW.
THE ONLY WAY PAST
IS TO PLOW STRAIGHT ON THROUGH.
FIRST MOVIE I SEE,
YOU'RE NOT ALONG.
FIRST TIME I HEAR
OUR FAVORITE SONG.

SLOWLY BUT SURELY,
I'M GAINING CONTROL.
BUT I'VE LOST MY TASTE
FOR DOVER SOLE.

*(Without allowing for applause, music segues immediately into song **HEADLIGHTS/TAIL LIGHTS**. Setting changes over intro.)*

Scene Five: The Visit

(FRAMED BACKGROUND PHOTO: Messy family room. All four actors enter frenetically, carrying various items to prepare for grandchildren's visit. Blow-up mattress, laundry basket full of toys, bags of candy, and stack of board games are among the items. There is constant chatter. A choreographed number.)

(A car screeching to a halt is heard.)

MAN ONE. Too late.

SONG: (5) "HEADLIGHTS-TAIL LIGHTS"

ALL.

THE GRANDKIDS ARE COMING '
HEY LOOK DOWN THE STREET

WOMAN ONE.

HI TIMMY

MAN TWO.

HI TAMMY

ALL.

WE'RE IN FOR A TREAT

WOMAN TWO.

CAN'T WAIT FOR THIS VISIT
IT'S GONNA BE SWELL

ALL.

A LITTLE LIKE HEAVEN

MAN TWO.

A LITTLE MORE LIKE HELL.

WOMAN TWO. *(spoken:)* Ralph!

ALL.

HEADLIGHTS TAIL LIGHTS
COMING AROUND
WE LOVE THE HUGS AND THE KISSES
AND THEIR WONDERFUL-WONDERFUL SOUND
HEADLIGHTS, TAIL LIGHTS
WE'RE SO OVERJOYED

MAN ONE.

> IN TWO HOURS FLAT
> OUR HOME WILL BE DESTROYED
>
> *(They clammer.)*

WOMAN ONE.

> MY DAUGHTER RELAXES
> LIKE WHEN SHE WAS YOUNG

MAN ONE.

> SHE LEAVES HER GUM ON MY FAXES
> AND HER CLOTHES ALL UNHUNG

WOMAN ONE.

> HER HUSBAND'S A GOOD GUY
> HE'S PLOWING AHEAD

MAN ONE.

> A REAL GOOD CHARMER
> WHO'S ALWAYS IN THE RED

WOMAN TWO. *(spoken:)* Think positive, Sweetie!

ALL.

> HEADLIGHTS TAIL LIGHTS
> NEVER A STRESS
> IT'S SUCH A WARM FUZZY FEELING
> AS WE'RE PICKING UP AFTER THEIR MESS
> HEADLIGHTS TAIL LIGHTS
> WE BASK IN THEIR GLOW

WOMAN TWO.

> THEIR PARENTS NEVER TAUGHT THEM
> THAT DON'T DO THAT MEANS "NO"

MAN ONE.

> THAT LIITLE GUY OF MINE
> I LIKE TO TAKE HIM BATTING
> AND IMPROVE HIS SWING

WOMAN ONE.

> THAT LITTLE GIRL OF MINE
> I COOK HER MY BEST MEALS
> BUT SHE WON'T EAT A THING

(A loud burst of thunder is heard.)

ALL.

LET'S GET OUT THE BOARD GAMES
THE FORECAST SAYS RAIN

MAN TWO.

PERHAPS IF IT THUNDERS
WE WON'T HEAR THEM COMPLAIN

ALL.

WE REALLY DO LOVE 'EM
THOUGH THEY DRIVE US BERSERK

MAN ONE/MAN TWO.

I PREFER TO JUST LOVE 'EM
AND NEVER DO THE WORK

ALL.

HEADLIGHT TAIL LIGHTS
BRIDGING THE GAP
WE LOVE EVERY MINUTE

WOMAN ONE.

ESPECIALLY THE MINUTE THEY NAP

ALL.

HEADLIGHTS TAIL LIGHTS
THE GOOD AND THE BAD

MAN ONE.

MY BODY ACHES IN PLACES I NEVER KNEW I HAD!

ALL.

WE LOVE IT WHEN THEY COME
WE GET TO PLAY GAMES
WE LOVE IT WHEN THEY COME

MAN TWO.

THOUGH I CAN NEVER REMEMBER THEIR NAMES

ALL.

WE LOVE IT WHEN THEY COME
IT'S PURE HEAVEN BLISS
WE LOVE IT WHEN THEY COME
LOVE TO GIVE THEM THEIR KISS
AND PACK THEM WITH THEIR
BOOKS AND TOYS AND SEND THEM

WOMAN ONE.

    NORTH BOUND,

MAN ONE.

    SOUTH BOUND,

WOMAN TWO.

    EAST BOUND,

MAN TWO.

    WEST BOUND,

ALL.

    AND PUT THEM UP ON A JUST FOUND
    SOLID GROUND, WRAP AROUND,
    OUT BOUND GREYHOUND BUS
    AND SEND THOSE TOO CUTE DARLINGS
    HOME...........WARD............. BOUND.

    (Red tail lights flash.)

WOMAN TWO. *(Spoken:)* Oh, I miss them already!

Scene Six: The Happy Couple

(FRAMED BACKGROUND PHOTO: "SECRETS TO A HAPPY MARRIAGE RETREAT" is displayed in the framed background photo. A podium is downstage right with a wine bottle and a glass of wine exposed. **MAN ONE,** *the* **ANNOUNCER,** *enters and speaks to the audience.)*

MAN ONE (ANNOUNCER). Ladies and Gentlemen, Pinehurst Community Center proudly presents Robert and Judy Marans: your hosts and experts on love and marriage. Now please, lets welcome them properly.

(Music: Fanfare.)

*(***MAN ONE*** exits.)*

*(***MAN TWO (BOB)*** *and* ***WOMAN TWO (JUDY)*** *enter excitedly and greet the audience from different sides of the stage. They are overly enthusiastic, even a bit tipsy. [Optional Minnesota accent for both.] Simultaneously, the exchange pleasantries with the audience, making small conversation: "Thank you for coming," "How was the traffic," etc., until* ***JUDY*** *calls for* ***BOB****'s attention.)*

JUDY (WOMAN TWO). Bob.

BOB (MAN TWO). What?

(She motions for him to come over to the podium where she is now standing.)

BOB. Oh, *(giggles)* I got to go. She's calling me.
Well, welcome, to the first annual, SECRETS OF A,

BOTH. *(with finger quotes)* "HAPPY MARRIAGE"

JUDY. *(with finger quotes)* "RETREAT."

BOB. Oh yea, *(finger quotes)* "Retreat." *(nervous laugh)* brought to you by the AMERICAN WINE ASSOCIA-TION.

(Both reach for the wine glass. ***JUDY*** *gets it first, leaving* ***BOB*** *to hold up the bottle instead.)*

JUDY. And thank you, American Wine Association.

(She takes a sip. He gives a nervous laugh.)

That's good stuff!

BOB. Now, I'm Robert Marans–

JUDY. Bob.

BOB. Bob. And this is my bride of thirty years, my Judy.

JUDY. *(She excitedly waves.)* Hi!

BOB. Now, we know that there have been numerous *(finger quotes)* "lectures," and "guidebooks" written, on…

BOTH. *(finger quotes)* "How to have a happy marriage."

JUDY. But we've decided to cut through the malarkey and give you the facts.

BOB. Why don't you start, my dear?

JUDY. Okee-dokey.

(She sings, while he listens with a smile.)

SONG: (6) "IF YOU WANT TO STAY MARRIED"

JUDY.

IF YOU WANT TO STAY MARRIED
IGNORE HIS SOCKS ON THE FLOOR
HOW HE NEVER HOLDS OPEN THE DOOR
AND THE WAY THAT HE SITS ALL DAY LONG ON SUNDAY
SWITCHING CHANNELS –
THESE ARE THE THINGS
THAT WILL DRIVE YOU INSANE
BUT YOU MUST NOT COMPLAIN
IF YOU WANT TO STAY MARRIED

(She takes another sip.)

BOB.

IF YOU WANT TO STAY MARRIED
GET USED TO HER BEING LATE
HOW SHE CONSTANTLY WATCHES HER WEIGHT
HOW SHE SPENDS TOO MUCH TIME IN THE BATHROOM
PUTTING ON HER MAKE-UP –
THESE ARE THE THINGS THAT'LL AGGRAVATE MEN
SO YOU JUST COUNT TO TEN
IF WE WANT TO STAY MARRIED

JUDY.

DON'T BOTHER TO THINK YOU CAN CHANGE THE PERSON
DON'T EVEN BOTHER TO TRY

BOB.

THE TRAITS THAT THEY HAVE OVER TIME GET WORSE

(He takes the glass of wine from her.)

JUDY.

AND YOU'LL NEVER QUITE SEE EYE TO EYE

BOB.

SHE ALWAYS LIKES TO GET DRESSED UP

JUDY.

HE'S JUST A BIG OLD GROUCH

BOB.

SO WE ARGUE AND SQUEAL

JUDY.

BUT THEN STRIKE UP A DEAL

BOTH.

'CAUSE WHO WANTS TO SLEEP ON THE COUCH?

(They hug.)

BOB.

IF YOU WANT TO STAY MARRIED
GET USED TO ALL OF HER SHOES

JUDY.

HOW HE SNORES

BOB.

HOW SHE YACKS ON AND ON WHILE SHE CHEWS

JUDY.

HOW HE MESSES UP ALL OF THE DRAWERS

BOB.

HOW SHE ALWAYS EXPECTS ME TO CLEAN THE KITCHEN

JUDY.

STOP YOUR BITCHIN'

(behind clenched teeth)

BOTH.

> THESE ARE THE THINGS THAT CAN DRIVE YOU TO DRINK
> BUT YOU DON'T MAKE A STINK
> IF YOU WANT TO STAY MARRIED

BOTH.

> YES, THESE ARE THE THINGS
> THAT DRIVE YOU UP A WALL
> BUT YOU'RE BETTER OFF
> SECRETLY CURSING
> AND QUIETLY SWEARING
> AND CORDIALLY SMILING
> AND SILENTLY GLARING
>
> *(She forcefully takes his arm.)*
>
> THAN NOT BEING MARRIED,

BOB. OW!

BOTH.

> AT ALL!
>
> *(They hug, take bows, and wave goodbye.)*

VOICE OVER: ANSWERING MACHINE. *(beep)*

GRANDMA. Hi my Darling. This is your mother calling. I'm so glad you and the children are coming for dinner Sunday night. I hope your husband is planning on staying longer than he did last week. Hugs and kisses. Bye-bye.

> *(beep)*

SON. Hi Dad, promise me you won't be mad – okay? Well, I came out of Starbucks today a little after five and found that they had towed my car away. Before you freak out the car is ABSOLUTELY FINE but obviously we'll need to discuss the ticket. We have insurance for that, right?

> *(beep)*

Scene Seven: Emily Goes to the Armani Store

(Music: Pre-recorded store music)

(FRAMED BACKGROUND PHOTO: Upscale women's clothing store. A clothing rack is exposed with Armani-merchandise. **MAN ONE (SALESMAN)** *is checking the merchandise.* **WOMAN ONE (EMILY**, *a new widow) and* **WOMAN TWO** *(her sister* **PAM***) enter.)*

PAM. Come along.

*(**PAM**, taking a hanger off the rack, holds it up for her* **EMILY***'s approval.)*

Do you like this?

EMILY. What's not to like?

PAM. It's ARMANI.

EMILY. It's who? *(She looks at a price tag.)* Pam, look at these prices!

PAM. Come on, Emily, would you like a Perrier?

EMILY. What do you mean? They sell it here?

PAM. No, they bring it to you. Do you want one or not?

EMILY. Pam…

PAM. What!

EMILY. I feel funny being here. I don't think it's right. Roger would not have approved. Let's go.

*(**EMILY** puts the jacket back on the rack and takes her sister's hand, trying hard to make an exit.* **PAM** resists.)*

PAM. *(calming her)* Emily, of course it's okay…How about this suit?

(holds up two blouses)

Do you like this blouse? Pick one.

(pause)

You'll try both. Okay, let's find…Sir…Sir, where are the fitting rooms?

SALESMAN. *(in snooty tone)* Here, let me take those from you, Madam.

EMILY. No, that's okay; I can carry them.

SALESMAN. That won't be necessary.

EMILY. No. I can!

(He tries to take them. She resists. It becomes a mini tug of war.)

PAM. Emily, give them to the man.

*(**SALESMEN** takes the clothes and gives her a snoot and walks past her to exit. **EMILY** gives the snoot right back to him behind his back.)*

EMILY. I don't know why you shop in stores like this.

PAM. *(dissapointed)* You know, sometimes it's very difficult to be your sister. This is supposed to be a fun outing.

EMILY. I know. I know. It's just that I never imagined myself in ARMANNY!

PAM. It's ARMANI.

EMILY. Potato, potahto.

(She spots a friend shopping at another counter.)

Oh my God, Pam, Stop…STOP…let me get behind you…no…just keep walking…keep your head down… WALK slowly-head down…SLOWER, I said…It's Donna!

PAM. So what if it's Donna?

EMILY. She can't see me here.

PAM. That's ridiculous. Let's go say hello.

*(**PAM** grabs **EMILY** by the hand and starts to walk towards the friend. **EMILY** pulls her back.)*

PAM. Oh come on. If she sees you here, then it's my fault. I dragged you here. It's me being an insensitive sister, okay? Will that make it easier?

EMILY. Don't be cute, and don't turn around. She'll notice. Just keep walking…and a little faster, please.

PAM. For Heaven's sake, Emily!

*(**EMILY** hides behind the rack and speaks through the clothes by parting them.)*

EMILY. If she sees me then she'll tell Sybil.

PAM. So what if Sybil knows?

EMILY. Well then if Sybil knows she'll tell Janice and Janice will tell Jackie and then...and then the whole city will know.

PAM. Will know what!?

EMILY. That I've been shopping at Armammy.

PAM. Yes, and...

EMILY. Three months after...

PAM. Where is it written that you can't go shopping three months after? Is there a mourner's manual I missed? I don't know where you got all this religion. It's hard to believe we were raised by the same parents.

EMILY. It's just not right to be shopping *here*!

PAM. Okay...according to your ancient manual, is it all right to go shopping at Bloomingdale's?

EMILY. There was no Bloomingdale's in Biblical times.

PAM. Okay, where is it written in this ancient book how many days after one could enter the town square? Did they have to wait to ride their camel?

EMILY. There are certain things...

PAM. How many months 'til you are allowed to go shopping?

EMILY. You should wait a decent interval.

PAM. What's a decent interval? Are there different rules that apply to different stores? Is it okay to go to the grocery store?

EMILY. You have to eat.

PAM. What about the drug store?

EMILY. That's okay if you're picking up a prescription.

PAM. T.J. Maxx?

EMILY. T.J. Maxx is acceptable IF I'm buying stuff for the grandchildren and just...because I...happen to be there I could pick up something for myself. BUT – my primary mission – something for the kids.

PAM. Okay, so it's not acceptable to think of one's self. Right?

EMILY. Right.

PAM. Is there a time period? When does it become acceptable? Six months? One year? One year and two months? One year three months and five days? Do holidays count? For God's sake, Emily!

EMILY. Pam, enough. Put it to bed. And don't turn around. She's back!

(**EMILY** *hides behind* **PAM.**)

PAM. What are you doing?!

EMILY. Where is she?

PAM. At the scarves. Go in the fitting room.

(**EMILY** *goes into an offstage fitting room and* **PAM** *sits outside and encourages her to try on everything. Pause.*)

PAM. How are you doing, Emily?

EMILY. Okay, but you keep an eye out for Donna and don't let her see you.

PAM. Okay, start trying. *(a pause)* What are you putting on first?

EMILY. *(She pokes her head out.)* I shouldn't be here…

PAM. Get back in there! I'll keep an eye out!

(*pause*)

What do you have on now?

(*another pause*)

EMILY. *(from offstage)* Oooh!

(**EMILY** *comes out in a pretty jacket.*)

Do you like this?

PAM. Oh my God! You look ten years younger in that jacket! It really shows off your figure!

EMILY. You think so? Maybe I should try it on with shoes.

(**SALESMAN** *pops out with shoes.*)

SALESMAN. Wa-lah! Here you go, Madam; I believe these are your size. Can I interest you in the purse they just unpacked in the back? It would be perfect with that outfit.

EMILY. Oh no. No thank you!

(**SALESMAN** *turns to walk away.*)

EMILY. Well, maybe.

SALESMAN. And there's some wonderful jewelry in the other room that they just marked down.

EMILY. Really!? Let's go. Come, Pam.

(**EMILY** *grabs* **PAM**'s *arm.*)

PAM. What happened to, "Roger wouldn't approve?"

EMILY. Rule number twelve of the mourners' manual: When presented with incredible couture – destroy manual. *(loudly)* Perrier please!

*(Playoff: **HEADLIGHTS / TAIL LIGHTS**)*

Scene Eight: Marvin

(FRAMED BACKGROUND PHOTO: Blank)

SONG: (7) "DOCTORS" REPRISE

MARVIN.

> WHEN YOU GOT AN ITCH
> WHICH BECOMES A RASH
> AND YOU SIT AND WATCH TV
> ANOTHER RERUN OF 'MASH'
> AND IT'S GETTING WORSE
> FROM YOUR POINT OF VIEW
> WHO DO YOU CALL?
> DOCTORS, THAT'S WHO

(speaking to the audience, stage left:)

My golf has definitely improved, but that's when my carpal tunnel syndrome started up again. So my orthopedist sent me to Dr. Green, a hand specialist. Now, hand specialists don't have a special name for themselves like my dermatologist, cardiologist or urologist does, but boy, are they special! His waiting room was packed.

(Crosses to stage right, sits down at edge of stage. While talking to the audience he takes off his shoe, exposing the ball of his foot.)

I ended up talking to a nice guy, about my age, and I mentioned that I also had this pain in the ball of my foot, and he said he has that same problem. Can you imagine – sitting right next to me?! Until you've had some physical condition yourself, you're usually unaware that almost everyone else you know, or their brother neighbor or cousin has had the same condition! And that's great, because then you can compare doctors.

(start playoff music)

NURSE. Marvin Maxwell

MARVIN. Over here.

NURSE. Please follow me.
MARVIN. Yay!

(music button)

Scene Nine: Cheap Spot

(FRAMED BACKGROUND PHOTO: A neighborhood restaurant. **MAN ONE [DAVE]** *enters with* **WOMAN TWO [SARA]**. *They check their coats.)*

DAVE. Where is Fred? I told him the prix fixe dinner stops at six.

SARA. Just relax.

DAVE. *(looking at his watch)* I wonder what's keeping him?

*(***JON** *and* **KARIN** *enter and greet* **DAVE** *and* **SARA**.*)*

DAVE. You're late.

FRED. I couldn't find a parking space.

DAVE. They have valet parking right in front.

KARIN. Don't even go there. We've been driving around for twenty minutes looking for a spot, as usual.

FRED. Karin, don't start up. *(He helps her out of her coat.)* Would you like to check your coat?

KARIN. No, I'll keep it.

FRED. Why don't you check your coat? You'll be more comfortable.

KARIN. I said, I'll keep it.

DAVE. Dinner is going to now cost us three hundred dollars – *(He throws a dirty look to* **FRED***.)* thanks to you – *(to* **KARIN***)* and she won't check your coat. *(to* **SARA***)* My sister is getting cheap in her old age.

SARA. Cheap? Look whose talking? Who rinses out plastic bags, turns them inside out to dry and then reuses them?

(All except **DAVE** *enjoy a chuckle.)*

DAVE. You got me there.

FRED. You know what my mom used to call that: a cheap spot. We all have them. It has nothing to do with actually being cheap. It's just that one little expense that bugs you.

KARIN. You got that right.

FRED. Some of the finest people I know have them. You should meet our neighbor.

SONG: (8) "EVERYONE'S GOT A CHEAP SPOT"

FRED.

MISTER CLARK IS A SUCCESSFUL LAWYER
OWNS TWO HOUSES AND THE LATEST MODEL CAR
GIVES HIS TIME AND ENERGY TO EVERY WORTHY CAUSE
HE'S MORE GENEROUS AND CARING
THAN MOST PEOPLE ARE.

TOOK HIS FRIENDS FOR DINNER AT A STEAKHOUSE
AND INSISTED ON PICKING UP THE TAB
THEN TUCKED HIS PANTS INTO SOCKS
AND HIKED THIRTY CITY BLOCKS
CAUSE HE WOULDN'T SPRING THE MONEY FOR CAB.

JUST PROVING...
EVERYBODY'S GOT A CHEAP SPOT
WHEN IT COMES TO SPENDING CASH
LIKE TO KEEP IT IN YOUR POCKET
BETTER YET, A SAFE AND LOCK IT
YOU NEVER KNOW WHEN THERE WILL BE A MARKET CRASH

SAVING ALL YOUR HARD EARNED DOLLARS
OFTEN TIME MAKES NO SENSE
YES, EVERYBODY'S GOT A CHEAP SPOT
SO HAVE A LAUGH AT YOUR OWN EXPENSE

KARIN. Actually, not checking coats is probably my only cheap spot.

FRED. What do you mean? You tear paper toweling in half.

SARA. You should buy the new select-a-size-half sheets.

FRED. She tears those in half.

KARIN. If you think I'm bad...

MY SISTER OWNS THE FINEST CHINA.
STERLING SILVER, STUBEN CRYSTAL,
ALL THE BEST!
PLANNED A GOURMET DINNER
JUST TO DAZZLE ALL HER FRIENDS
ADDING FLOWERS TO THE FOYER
TO IMPRESS EACH GUEST...

KARIN. *(cont.)*

> WE ARRIVED AT SEVEN JUST TO HELP HER
> AND THE SETTING WAS WHAT YOU DREAM ABOUT
> I BEGAN TO LIGHT A CANDLE
> WHEN SHE FLEW RIGHT OFF THE HANDLE
> SCREAMING, "NO ONES HERE YET
> BLOW THOSE CANDLES OUT!"
> JUST PROVING...

FRED & KARIN.

> EVERYONE'S GOT A CHEAP SPOT
> IT'S THAT DEEP DOWN, NUMBING CHILL
> NOT A SOUL AROUND CAN HIDE IT
> AND I'VE KNOWN A LOT WHO'VE TRIED IT.
> IT'S THAT NERVOUSNESS THAT COMES
> EACH TIME YOU GET THE BILL.
> SAVING ALL YOUR HARD EARNED PENNIES
> ISN'T A BAD OFFENSE,
> 'CAUSE EVERYBODY'S GOT A CHEAP SPOT
> SO HAVE A LAUGH AT YOUR OWN EXPENSE.

DAVE. Wait, I got one!

> MISTER JONES LOVES SPENDING ON HIS GRANDKIDS
> PAYS FOR PRIVATE SCHOOL
> AND SUMMER CAMP EACH YEAR
> IT'S HIS PLEASURE BUYING THINGS
> FOR EVERYONE HE LOVES
> HE ALWAYS KEEPS HIS CREDIT CARD
> AND CHECKBOOK NEAR.
>
> GAVE THE GANG A FIRST CLASS TRIP TO NAPLES
> ADDED TO IT, A CARRIBEAN CRUISE
> BUT HE HAD A PAINFUL TIME
> CAUSE HE WOULDN'T SPEND A DIME
> ON A DECENT PAIR

(+SARA)

> OF PROPER WALKING SHOES.

DAVE.

> JUST PROVING...

ALL.

EVERYBODY'S GOT A CHEAP SPOT
THERE'S NO REASON TO PRETEND
IT CAN SURFACE UNEXPECTED
BECAUSE EVERYONE'S AFFECTED
BY THAT LITTLE VOICE INSIDE THAT TELLS YOU,
"DO NOT SPEND"

FOR A LIFE THAT'S FREE FROM WORRY
NEVERMIND FEELING TENSE
'CAUSE, EVERYBODY'S GOT A CHEAP SPOT.
SO HAVE A LAUGH
HA HA HA HA HA HA HA HA
AT YOUR OWN EXPENSE.

(music playoff)

Scene Ten: Computer Dating

(FRAMED BACKGROUND PHOTO: Home Office. **WOMAN ONE [EMILY]** *and* **WOMAN TWO [GIRL-FRIEND]** *are at a computer, stage right.)*

EMILY. What does the "J" stand for?

GIRLFRIEND. Jewish.

EMILY. A Jewish dating site? But I'm not Jewish!

GIRLFRIEND. No, but the men are. It's a known fact they make the best husbands.

EMILY. I liked it better the old fashioned way.

GIRLFRIEND. Like you married whomever you were dating at 20? We didn't know what we were doing.

EMILY. Speak for yourself. I married Roger for two important reasons.

GIRLFRIEND. Yeah, what were they?

EMILY. He was cute, and I wanted to buy dishes.

GIRLFRIEND. Come on, Emily, my neighbor's cousin found a great guy on this site. I'm going to help you get started. Let's see…oh, here it is. We have to create a profile. Name?… NAME?

EMILY. I'm not doing this.

(FRAMED BACKGROUND PHOTO: switches to Michael's living room. Lights down on women and lights up on **MEN** *stage left.* **MAN ONE** *is* **MICHAEL,** **MAN TWO** *is his* **FRIEND**.*)*

MICHAEL. I'm not doing this!

FRIEND. Right. Don't do this, Michael. Just stay in your house. Keep the curtains drawn and watch re-runs of Bonanza.

MICHAEL. Bonanza was good.

FRIEND. Michael, they're all dead. What does it tell you when you prefer keeping company with flat dead people instead of round live ones?

MICHAEL. Round?

FRIEND. Women. Remember them?

MICHAEL. I don't remember them. I remember her.

FRIEND. Katie's gone and you're here. Don't get all past tense when you're still in the present.

MICHAEL. Aw, who would be interested in me?

FRIEND. Okay, let's get started. NAME...Let's call you... Tony.

MICHAEL. My name is Michael.

FRIEND. No one uses their real name. Okay Tony, let's see...

(Lights down on MEN, *lights up on* WOMEN.*)*

GIRLFRIEND. NAME.

EMILY. You know. Emily Anderson.

GIRLFRIEND. NAME. Trixy. That's a good name.

EMILY. Trixy? What are you doing?

GIRLFRIEND. Interests. What do you like to do?

EMILY. I like to garden and knit.

GIRLFRIEND. Likes to bike ride and rock climb.

EMILY. Great, I'll climb the Matterhorn and knit the flag on top.

GIRLFRIEND. Children?...How many children?

EMILY. You know, three.

GIRLFRIEND. No Children. Men are looking for one relationship not four.

(Lights down on WOMEN, *lights up on* MEN.*)*

FRIEND. Okay Tony, time for a photo. Do you have one?

MICHAEL. No.

FRIEND. Then I'll take one.

(He pulls out his camera phone.)

Smile.

(takes a picture on his cell phone and looks at it)

This looks pretty good.

MICHAEL. Let me see.

(He looks at it.)

Looks like an ad for Polident. Take another. This time I won't smile.

FRIEND. *(He takes another picture.)* How's this Michael?

MICHAEL. It looks like I should be holding up a number in front of my chest. Forget the photo.

(Lights down on **MEN,** *lights up on* **WOMEN.)**

GIRLFRIEND. Okay, Emily, I mean Trixy. Describe yourself.

EMILY. Let's see…I have long blond hair and I'm 5'8.

GIRLFRIEND. Since when are you 5'8"?

EMILY. Since I've had long blond hair?

(Lights down on **WOMEN,** *lights up on* **MEN.)**

FRIEND. Describe yourself.

MICHAEL. Closet sex maniac.

FRIEND. All right, Travolta. Forget it, we'll move on. What are you interests, Mister Tony?

MICHAEL. Oh, gardening, fishing. Oh, and sci-fi novels.

FRIEND. That's what I like about you Michael – sociable kind of guy.

(typing)

Let's put in Tony likes biking, rock climbing and musical theater.

MICHAEL. What?

FRIEND. You wanna find someone, don't cha?

MICHAEL. Yes, I want to find someone who will share my REAL interests. I can't even name a musical theater show!

FRIEND. You remember. *Guys and Dolls* – high school?

MICHAEL. *(sings)*

LUCK BE A LADY TONIGHT.

(Lights down on **MEN,** *lights up on* **WOMEN.)**

EMILY. *(She sings.)*

   'I'LL KNOW WHEN MY LOVE COMES ALONG.'

GIRLFRIEND. Do you really want to put in, 'Musical Theater?"

EMILY. You asked for my interests.

GIRLFRIEND. Let's put in action movies. Now Trix, what do you like to read?

EMILY. Jane Austen, The New Yorker, a little Shakespeare.

GIRLFRIEND. Jackie Collins, Stephen King, People Magazine.

(Lights down on **WOMEN**, *lights up on* **MEN**.*)*

MICHAEL. Sherlock Holmes, The New Yorker, and Stephen King

FRIEND. Likes to read: Managing Your Wealth, Wine Spectator, and People Magazine.

   Moving on. Likes and dislikes. Do you like to travel?

MICHAEL. Not alone.

(Lights up on two **WOMEN**.*)*

GIRLFRIEND. Do you like dogs?

EMILY. I've dated enough of them. This whole thing is stupid. Why can't I just tell the truth.

(Lights down on **WOMEN**, *lights up on* **MEN**.*)*

MICHAEL. Why can't I just tell the truth?

FRIEND. Because that's just not how it's done, my friend! Imagine that somewhere, somebody is reading this. They're gonna be thinking: "Managing Your Wealth, athletic…this guy's a real catch!"

(Lights down on **MEN**, *lights up on* **WOMEN**.*)*

GIRLFRIEND. They're gonna be thinking: "Here's a gal who likes to bike and hike and has no children. What a catch." Ready to submit? *(She gives one final click of the mouse.)* To new beginnings.

(Lights up on all.)

FRIEND. *(one final click of the mouse)* To finding new love. You wanna go get a beer?

MICHAEL. Make it a keg.

GIRLFRIEND. You wanna go to Cosco?

EMILY. Make it Neiman Marcus.

(Music playoff a la Guys and Dolls)

Scene Eleven: Stuck In the Middle

(FRAMED BACKGROUND PHOTO: A backyard setting. **MAN ONE (JOEY)** *wearing an apron is grilling on a Weber Grill.)*

JOEY. My momma, who lives with us, is 92. My youngest daughter, Mary Jo, 18, is home for the summer. And they're both driving me nuts. I'm takin' care of Mom, and still supportin' my daughter, which I guess makes me one of the Sandwich Generation.

SONG: (9) "SANDWICH GENERATION"

WHEN MY MOTHER TURNED NINETY SHE BEGAN TO
    UNWIND
AND DO AS SHE PLEASES, SAY WHATEVER'S ON HER MIND.
MY DAUGHTER IS BITTER, AS TEENAGERS ARE
SHE DOESN'T DO NUTTIN', YET SHE WANTS A NEW CAR.

A scooter maybe.

MY MOM'S ALWAYS FREEZING, TURNS THE THERMOSTAT
    HIGH
SHE'LL PUT ON A SWEATER IN THE MIDDLE OF JULY
THEN MY DAUGHTER SAYS SHE'S ROASTING, AND TURNS UP
    THE A.C.
AND MY WIFES HAVING HOT FLASHES, 'CAUSE SHE'S 53.

I'M THE SANDWICH, THE SANDWICH,
THE SANDWICH GENERATION
AND I'M SICK OF GIVING ALL THE LIVING LONG DAY.
IT'S THE HEADACHES, THE HEARTACHES, THE PAIN AND
    AGGRAVATION
AND IT'S CONSTANT AS BEES COME IN MAY

(He swats at bees around his head with his spatula.)

(spoken) Can't get a word in edgewise!

MY DAUGHTER PLAYS MUSIC, AS LOUD AS SHE CAN
IT DISTURBS ALL THE NEIGHBORS, BUT I GUESS THAT'S THE
    PLAN.
MY MOTHER CAN'T HEAR IT, DON'T CARE IF IT'S PLAYED
SHE JUST TURNS DOWN THE VOLUME ON HER HEARING AID

JOEY. *(cont.)*

> AND I'M THE SANDWICH, THE SANDWICH,
> THE SANDWICH GENERATION
> AND I'M SICK OF GIVING ALL THE LIVING LONG DAY.
> IT'S THE HEADACHES, THE HEARTACHES, THE PAIN AND
> AGGRAVATION
> AND WHAT HAIR I GOT LEFT 'S TURNIN' GREY
>
> IT'S MORNIN' TIL NIGHTTIME, AND WEEK AFTER WEEK
> THEY'RE BITCHIN' AND GROANIN' EVEN NOW AS WE SPEAK
> BUT OF ALL OF THE SAYINGS THE BEST THAT I'VE HEARD
> IS "JUST KEEP YOUR MOUTH SHUT AND DON'T SAY A
> WORD."
>
> YES, I'M THE SANDWICH, THE SANDWICH,
> THE SANDWICH GENERATION
> AND I'M SICK OF GIVING ALL THE LIVING LONG DAY.
> IT'S THE HEADACHES, THE HEARTACHES, THE PAIN AND
> AGGRAVATION
> BUT...
> I WOULDN'T HAVE IT ANY OTHER WAY.
> NO, I WOULDN'T HAVE IT ANY OTHER WAY.

Scene Twelve: Wedding Reception

(FRAMED BACKGROUND PHOTO: Wedding Reception. **WOMAN TWO (ELAINE)** *and* **MAN TWO** *(her ex-husband* **PETER***). They are both in party clothes and enter separately. They are each awkwardly munching on pieces of wedding cake – not looking at each other.)*

PETER. So what did you give them, a punch bowl? You gave them a punch bowl, didn't you?

ELAINE. No, I didn't give them a punch bowl.

PETER. You always give punch bowls. Every time there's a wedding – the punch bowl.

ELAINE. Well I didn't do it this time!

PETER. If I had known you weren't going to, I would have!

ELAINE. Is that my fault?

PETER. I didn't say it was your fault; I'm just saying I'm blaming you. *(a beat)* So what did you get them?

ELAINE. Something they were registered for… You didn't bring the girlfriend?

PETER. What is she going to do here? Everyone is twenty-five years older than she is.

ELAINE. Only 25? Are you still an item?

PETER. I bet we have four or five other topics we could discuss.

ELAINE. I'm sure you're right but I'm tired of 'small-talk.'

PETER. I'm merely saying you're too direct. If you want to know the status of my relationship, we talk and you infer from what I'm not saying.

ELAINE. Sorry to hear that.

PETER. I haven't said anything yet.

ELAINE. I'm a quick inferrer.

PETER. What should I infer about you and what's his name? How's it going?

ELAINE. It went. Let me rephrase – he went.

PETER. No!

ELAINE. Tell me this is a surprise and I'll pretend to believe you. And you can pretend you're sorry for me and I'll pretend right back to you. Here we are again both pretending. *(a beat)* Not that different from when we were married.

PETER. What if I tell you I'm not pretending?

ELAINE. About what?

PETER. Caring.

(He motions she has something on her face. She lifts her napkin and wipes the side of her mouth but misses completely.)

ELAINE. Did I get it?

(Leaning forward with his own cocktail napkin, he cleans off the spot. His hand stops for a moment on her cheek. Their eyes lock for an instant. He nervously pulls away.)

Were you going to ask me to dance?

PETER. Were you going to say yes?

ELAINE. Try me.

PETER. Consider yourself asked.

ELAINE. You always could lay on the charm.

(Music is being softly played in the background. They get up to dance to the music. The music comes to a finish.)

PETER. Would you like to get out of here and go for a drink?

ELAINE. Sure.

SONG: (10) "IT'S NOT A DATE"

PETER.
SHE'S LOOKING GOOD

ELAINE.
HE'S LOST SOME WEIGHT.

PETER.
IT'S JUST A DRINK
IT'S NOT A DATE

ELAINE.

> I'M ONLY GOING
> 'CAUSE I KNOW HE NEEDS ME SO

PETER.

> WE'LL TAKE A WALK
> STROLL BY THE LAKE

ELAINE.

> IT'S NOT AS THOUGH
> SOMETHING'S AT STAKE

PETER.

> I'M ONLY GOING 'CAUSE I KNOW
> SHE NEEDS ME SO

ELAINE.

> BUT I CAN TELL
> HE'S AT LOOSE ENDS

PETER.

> OH, WHAT THE HELL
> CAN'T WE BE FRIENDS?

BOTH.

> NOBODY ELSE WOULD UNDERSTAND MY WOUNDED PRIDE.

ELAINE.

> I SHOULDN'T CARE
> IT'S NOT AS THOUGH
> WE'RE STILL A PAIR

BOTH.

> BUT EVEN SO
> I KNOW HOW (HE/SHE) CAN HOLD (HIS/HER) PAIN
> DEEP DOWN INSIDE.

> *(They speak to each other.)*

PETER. We have to say our 'goodbyes' to our hosts. And we can't do it together.

ELAINE. Let's wait a few minutes then I'll start with the bride's mother and you take the father; then we'll switch. Our relatives have talked about us enough.

PETER. I'm not here for their entertainment.

ELAINE. I think your cousin has spotted us.

PETER. Damn.

ELAINE.

LET'S GET OUR COATS

PETER.

OUTSIDE WE'LL MEET

ELAINE.

LET ME GO FIRST

PETER.

YEAH THAT'S DISCREET

BOTH.

WHAT HARM CAN COME
A SIMPLE DRINK

ELAINE.

IT'S JUST A NIGHT

(back to internal monologue)

WHAT COULD IT HURT?
I KNOW HIS WAYS

PETER.

I'LL DRIVE HER HOME

ELAINE.

I HOPE HE STAYS

BOTH.

MAYBE THIS TIME,
WITH ALL I'VE LEARNED,
I'LL GET IT RIGHT.
MAYBE THIS TIME,
WITH ALL WE'VE LEARNED
WE'LL GET IT RIGHT.

Scene Thirteen: Time Moves On...

SONG: (11) "NOW WHAT?" REPRISE

WOMAN ONE.

TIME MOVES ON AND WE HAVEN'T GOT A CLUE

MAN ONE.

AROUND EVERY CORNER IS SOMETHING STRANGE AND NEW

WOMAN TWO/MAN TWO.

TIME MOVES ON LOVE CAN DISAPPEAR SO FAST

ALL.

AND MAYBE WITH TIME WE CAN LEARN FROM THE PAST.

Scene Fourteen: Marvin

(Marvin 'play-on' music)

(FRAMED BACKGROUND PHOTO: Blank.)

SONG: (12) "DOCTORS" REPRISE

MARVIN.

WHEN YOUR BODY'S STIFF
OH IT'S SUCH A CURSE
WHEN YOUR JOINTS ARE TENSE AND TIGHT
IT'S LIKE ARTHRITUS BUT WORSE
WHEN YOU HEAR YOUR KNEES
SCREAMING, "NO CAN DO"
WHO DO YOU CALL? DOCTORS, THAT'S WHO

(greeting an audience member)

Hey, did I mention Dr. Sandy? *(gives him a business card)* No one does a colonoscopy like he does! Speaking of assholes.

(rimshot or piano)

Oh look, there goes my neighbor, Rick. He's out there, rain or shine. To me, getting in and out of a golf cart for two hours is exhausting. I've been trying to wait out this 'exercise craze', but it doesn't seem to be going away. Rick even has one of those Pilates machines, which to me has a lot in common with the torture devices used during the Spanish Inquisition. He not only exercises, he's a health nut – whatever that means. When I was growing up, Wonder bread was good for you. Cheese – very good for you. Red meat made you strong. Milk products – the more the better, and exercise – only if you wanted to do it for fun. Boy, have times changed. I'm trying to adapt but every so often I crave a double order of well-done French fries even though eating carbs is practically against federal law. And what's with everyone carrying around bottled water? What's next?! I need to go ponder this at Wendy's.

*(Music button, **MARVIN** skips off to music.)*

Scene Fifteen: It's Not My Fault!

(FRAMED BACKGROUND PHOTO: An Office. **WOMAN TWO** *(a well-dressed* **CLIENT***) enters wearing dark glasses and a headscarf practically covering her face. She sits at a desk chair waiting for* **MAN ONE** *(***INSURANCE ADJUSTER***) to enter. He enters.)*

INSURANCE ADJUSTER. Miss McNair, Consolidated Health Insurance is not trying to shirk its responsibilities. Your policy covers keeping you in good physical health due to conditions beyond your control.

CLIENT (WOMAN TWO). Then we agree.

INSURANCE ADJUSTER. Pardon me?

CLIENT. My problems are due to conditions beyond my control. These tiny lines around my eyes – Watergate. These flabby arms *(She wiggles her flab.)* – the Gulf war. The market dropped and so did *(lifts up her boobs and lets them drop)* these. Hot flashes – global warming.

INSURANCE ADJUSTER. I think that's a stretch.

CLIENT. No, the stretch marks are over here *(points to stomach)* caused by inflation. Why couldn't inflation happen here *(points back to boob)*

INSURANCE ADJUSTER. Miss McNair, your policy covers keeping your lungs and heart and colon in good repair, and we here at Consolidated Health Insurance have a well-established reputation and we pride ourselves for being fair.

CLIENT. Then live up to that reputation. I've been paying your premiums for years and luckily for you I haven't needed to collect because my problems have been slow growing.

INSURANCE ADJUSTER. Slow – growing?

CLIENT. *(removing her scarf and dark glasses)* Do you think this happened overnight!?

INSURANCE ADJUSTER. I'm sorry, ma'am. You simply do not have a case.

CLIENT. How can you say that? Just look at me!

SONG: (13) "I GOT A CASE"

CLIENT.

I GOT A CASE

I GOT A CASE

THERE WAS A TIME WHEN MEN CONSIDERED ME A HOTTIE

NOW WHAT THIS GOVERNMENT'S INFLICTED ON MY BODY'S
A DISGRACE

I GOT A CASE.

INSURANCE ADJUSTER. I don't think you understand. We approve surgeries to…well, to keep away death.

CLIENT. But there's death and there's death.

INSURANCE ADJUSTER. I'm not sure I'm following…

CLIENT. I'm talking about social death.

INSURANCE ADJUSTER. Your policy doesn't cover social death. For that, Miss McNair, perhaps you should contact Dr. Phil.

CLIENT. Dr. Phil?! Let's sing it sisters!

(backup singers enter and sing with her)

I GOT A PLAN

I GOT A GOOD PLAN

WE'RE GONNA GET THESE TUBBY TUMMIES TUCKED AND
LIFTED

IT'S NOT OUR FAULT THE WORLD'S A MESS

AND THINGS HAVE SHIFTED OUT OF PLACE

WE GOT A CASE

(He's reviewing her chart.)

INSURANCE ADJUSTER. What you are describing is elective surgery. Optional…Non-essential…

CLIENT.

SEE THIS HANGING SAGGY SKIN

HAPPENED DURING NIXON'S REIGN

ONCE I HAD A PERFECT CHIN

NOW IT'S GONE

BLAME IT ON SARAH PALIN'S CAMPAIGN

I GOT A CASE

I GOT A CASE

THEN I'LL BE YOUNG AGAIN AND PURRING LIKE A KITTEN

WHEN THEY ERASE THE LINES OF HIST'RY THAT ARE
    WRITTEN ON MY FACE
I GOT A CASE

CLIENT. I am only asking approval for necessary procedures.

(reading from her file)

INSURANCE ADJUSTER. A face-lift?

CLIENT. Urgent!

INSURANCE ADJUSTER. A tummy tuck?

CLIENT. Crucial

INSURANCE ADJUSTER. And a mammary recalibration?

CLIENT. *(glancing down at her own boobs)*
MANDATORY!!!

By the way. I've known you for years and I've watched
what it's done to you.

INSURANCE ADJUSTER. Done to me? What are you talking
about?

CLIENT. I noticed your hair first starting to fall out? When
the Berlin Wall fell.

INSURANCE ADJUSTER. But that was a happy event.

CLIENT. But how many of your relatives were able to come
here because of that? What stress did that cause you?

INSURANCE ADJUSTER. Now that you mentioned it...

CLIENT. *(pulling up his trouser leg)*
SEE THESE UGLY SPIDER VEINS
RUSSIAN SHIPS AND J.F.K.

INSURANCE ADJUSTER.
ALL I GOT ARE ACHES AND PAINS

CLIENT.
WHICH OCCURED WHEN YOU LEARNED OF GUANTANAMO
    BAY

INSURANCE ADJUSTER. You know, you're right!

CLIENT.
YOU GOT A CASE

INSURANCE ADJUSTER.
WE GOT A CASE

BOTH.

> CAUSE WE'RE POLITICALLY BRUISED AND BATTERED
>   CREATURES
> WHO NEED TO GO AND GET THEIR BRUISED AND BATTERED
>   FEATURES
> BACK IN PLACE

CLIENT.

> WHY NOT!?

INSURANCE ADJUSTER.

> WHY NOT!?

BOTH.

> 'CAUSE THERE'S NO POINT IN DOIN' NUTTIN'
> I PREFER JUST CUTTIN' TO THE CHASE

INSURANCE ADJUSTER.

> CUTTIN HERE

> *(with hands lifts eyebrows)*

CLIENT.

> CUTTIN HERE

> *(pulls neck skin taught)*

INSURANCE ADJUSTER.

> CUTTIN THERE!

> *(points to her behind)*

CLIENT. Hey!

BOTH.

> WE GOT A DAMN GOOD, AIR TIGHT, FOOL PROOF, MOTHER
>   OF A CASE!

Scene Sixteen: Computer #2

(FRAMED BACKGROUND PHOTOS: Home offices of **WOMAN ONE (EMILY)** *and* **MAN ONE (MICHAEL)**. **WOMAN ONE (TRIX-EMILY)** *and* **MAN ONE (TONY-MICHAEL)** *are each in their own apartments on their computers.)*

SONG: (14) "THE CHAT"

MICHAEL (TONY).
> HI TRIX, I HOPE THIS FINDS YOU WELL.
> YOUR LISTING CAUGHT MY EYE RIGHT OFF THE BAT
> WE'VE GOT A LOT IN COMMON FAR AS I CAN TELL,
> SO I HOPE YOU HAVE A MOMENT FOR A CHAT.

EMILY (TRIX). Ooooh, intresting.
> HI TONY, NICE OF YOU TO WRITE
> I JUST GOT HOME FROM DINNER AND
> I'M STUCK HERE FOR THE NIGHT.
> MY FRIDAY PLANS HAVE FALLEN THROUGH
> SO TELL ME – WHAT'S NEW?

TONY. She's actually responding. Let's see…
> WELL THIS MORNING I WOKE UP
> AND IT WAS A PRETTY DAY
> SO I THOUGHT I'D DO SOME PRUNING IN THE YARD
> SO I GRABBED MY BRAND NEW SHEARS
> AND I HACKED SOME WEEDS AWAY AND I… …

(shakes his head and takes a deep breathe)

> DAMN IT THIS IS HARD!
> … …
> SO THIS MORNING I WOKE UP AND I HEADED FOR THE GYM
> WHERE I SET THE TREADMILL FOR A SIX MILE HIKE.
> THEN I RODE FOR TWENTY MILES ON THE BIKE.

TRIX.
> THAT SOUNDS LIKE A PRODUCTIVE DAY
> YOU MUST BE IN GREAT SHAPE I'D SAY.
> I ATTENDED MY NEW OPERA CLASS
> …*(spoken)* No…
> MY PILATES CLASS
> THEN I WENT TO SEE THE YANKEES PLAY.

TONY. Wow!

> I LIKE THE YANKEES
> YOU LIKE THE YANKEES
> WHAT A GREAT COINCIDENCE
> WE BOTH LIKE THE YANKEES
> BUT BASEBALL'S NOT MY ONE AND ONLY CARE
> I HAVE OTHER INTERESTS I CAN SHARE.

TRIX. Oh!

TONY.

> I LIKE OPERA

TRIX. Opera?

> AND THE BALLET
> AND AN EVENING OF BECKETT'S IDEAL
> I LIKE SHAKESPEARE AND HENRIK IBSEN
> BUT THERE'S NOTHING LIKE EUGENE O'NEILL

TRIX. Oh brother. A show off, huh? Let's see here.

TRIX.

> HAVE YOU SEEN THE NEW PRODUCTION OF
> THE ICEMAN COMETH
> PLAYING AT THE ATTIC RIGHT DOWNTOWN?
> I SAW THAT, IT GOT A GREAT REVIEW.

TONY.

> I DID TOO.
> THE SCENERY WAS SPECIAL
> THE ACTORS WERE DIVINE
> BUT THE LIGHTING AND THE SOUND WERE PRETTY
>   ROTTEN

TRIX.

> IT MIGHT SURPRISE YOU THEN TO KNOW
> IT WON'T OPEN 'TIL NEXT JUNE
> NOW THE ATTIC'S PLAYING, "MOON FOR THE
>   MISBEGOTTEN."

TONY. *(nervous laugh)* Well, two can play this game!

> THAT MAY VERY WELL BE TRUE
> BUT WHILE WE'RE TALKING RHYME AND REASON
> THE YANKEES AREN'T PLAYING, CAUSE IT'S FOOTBALL
>   SEASON!

TRIX.

I'VE GOT SOMETHING IN THE OVEN

TONY.

I'VE GOT ERRANDS TO DO

BOTH.

IT WAS VERY NICE CHATTING WITH YOU!

(They both close their computers.)

PRE-RECORDED VOICE OVER: ANSWERING MACHINE. *(beep)*

DAUGHTER. Hi, Mom. I'm bringing Steve home for dinner on Thursday. I can't wait for you to meet him. I've only known him for a month but I think he's the one. And don't listen to what Aunt Barbara said about him-trust me, you're gonna love him. Bye.

(beep)

Scene Seventeen: His Girl, Thursday

(FRAMED BACKGROUND PHOTO: An upscale grocery market. **WOMAN ONE (MISTRESS)** *meets* **WOMAN TWO (WIDOW)** *in a grocery store. They each carry shopping baskets, slightly filled.* **WIDOW** *is reading label on yogurt.* **MISTRESS** *is circling nervously.)*

MISTRESS. *(after a pause)* Check the date on that yogurt. This store's been cited for selling out-dated yogurt.

WIDOW. *(curt answers)* Thank you.

MISTRESS. *(after another pause.)* I only come here because I like the fruit. It's really good here.

WIDOW. Yes, I suppose they do have nice fruit.

MISTRESS. *(another pause.)* They've certainly updated this store.

WIDOW. *(glaring at her directly)* Competition's tough these days.

MISTRESS. Listen, I know you don't know who I am, but I thought you should know – your husband and I carried on an affair for fifteen years. Right up until his untimely death.

WIDOW. Edward shouldn't have been driving his Mercedes so fast. Go on.

MISTRESS. I came to his office as a temp way back when Ed was working for Barney Logan & Smith law firm. We started out as just friends. It was innocent enough. *(dramatically)* But late nights and long hours...well you know what happens. I tried to break it off numerous times, but well...he just wouldn't have it. I know this must come as a shock –

WIDOW. Not at all, I know exactly who you are. Can you hand me that cheese?

MISTRESS. What?! You couldn't possibly...

WIDOW. Yes, you're Cindy. But I like to call you Thursday. I ran into Tuesday last week at the hairdresser. Pretty young thing.

MISTRESS. I'm who?

WIDOW. You're Thursday. Thank you so much for being 'Thursday'. That's the night Ed would go visit you and I would have the house to myself. How do you like them apples? *(referring to actual apples)* I didn't have to come home early to cook dinner and entertain. That's the night I usually went to the modern art lectures. Ed never liked modern art but you must know that. *(rambling on)* I went to foreign films and chamber music. Ed never liked chamber music either – except Schubert. He was pissed when I went to hear it without him. I promised him I'd never go to hear Schubert on Thursdays, which was kind of complicated because I couldn't go on Tuesdays either.

MISTRESS. You knew about me?

WIDOW. How's your niece? Did that ingrown toenail ever work out?

MISTRESS. *(bewildered)* She's…fine, thank you.

WIDOW. We were concerned about that toenail. I know she wanted to be a foot model… Maybe she could model the other foot.

MISTRESS. This might not be the appropriate place to discuss such personal matters.

WIDOW. Ah, you mean you didn't come just to warn me about out-dated yogurt?

MISTRESS. I confess I saw you come in and I just had to tell you. There's a slight issue.

WIDOW. Pardon me? A slight issue? You didn't have Ed's baby?

MISTRESS. No. No.

WIDOW. Good 'cause calling that a slight issue – I might have thought you callous.

MISTRESS. Your husband has provided me for the last fifteen years with an apartment on Park Avenue, an unlimited Visa Gold card, and health club membership. We've gone on vacations to Aruba, and he sent me monthly to the Canyon Ranch Spa. And I gave up everything for him.

WIDOW. Yes…

MISTRESS. I feel I'm owed continued support to maintain the lifestyle to which I have become accustomed. *(slyly)* And knowing your husband's position, I'm sure the newspapers would be very interested in this story.

WIDOW. *(She bites into a grape.)* Boy, these grapes are sour. Oh, believe me. You're not telling me anything I didn't know. I selected that apartment myself!

MISTRESS. *(amazed)* You did?

WIDOW. It has a nice view don't you think? That is until that God-ugly building blocked your view of the East river. There wasn't much I could do about that.

MISTRESS. Look. I don't have a job and in this economy I don't intend to start looking for work. It would do real damage to your family's reputation if everybody knew.

WIDOW. STOP. Everybody knows. If you're worried about reputations, I would worry about *your* reputation.

MISTRESS. Why mine?

WIDOW. You might want to find another gentleman from say Ed's inner circle and if you don't act quickly you might have waited too long. Excuse me, would you check the date on that milk. It might be EXPIRED. Now, you might be getting some phone calls from some of these rich connected gentleman, especially if I put in a good word for you. But, on the other hand if they know you're after Ed's money…I mean, they'll all run for the hills. I'm just speaking out of concern for you. You're endangering your market value.

MISTRESS. You think you might know somebody who might be interested in me?

WIDOW. For all those wonderful free Thursdays, I think I owe you.

MISTRESS. *(dumbfounded)* Well…thank you.

WIDOW. I'm checking out. Give me a call me next week.

(She hand her a business card.)

MISTRESS. Hmm. Peachy! *(She tosses up a peach that she has been holding.)*

(They join arms and walk offstage.)

Scene Eighteen: Temptation

(FRAMED BACKGROUND PHOTO: Bar Scene. **WOMAN ONE (MELINDA)** *and* **MAN TWO (TED),** *at opposite sides of the stage at two bar tables.)*

SONG: (15) "PERFECT BLISS"

TED. *(to audience)*
I VALUE MY FAMILY
I WOULD NEVER CHEAT ON MY WIFE
ON A SCALE OF ONE TO TEN
I MARK NINE
FOR A DAMN GOOD LIFE.

MELINDA.
I'M ONE OF THE LUCKY GALS
'CAUSE I MARRIED THE GUY OF MY DREAMS
WE'RE THE PICTURE OF PERFECT BLISS BUT THEN,
NOTHING IS AS IT SEEMS

TED.
BORDOM SETS IN FROM TIME TO TIME
WHEN I THINK OF WHAT MIGHT HAVE BEEN

MELINDA.
I GOT CAUGHT IN THE THRILL OF THE MOMENT
LET'S SEE, WHERE DO I BEGIN?

*(***WOMAN TWO*** enters a sexy lady,* **MAN ONE** *enters as handsome gent. A choreographed number.)*

TED.
I'M ON A BUSINESS TRIP TO KENTUCKY
IT IS LATE I GO OUT FOR A BITE
THERE'S THIS GAL ALL ALONE AT A TABLE
SHE IS WEARING A DRESS KINDA TIGHT

MELINDA.
I'M OUT SHOPPING AND RAN INTO ANDREW
HE STILL LOOKS LIKE THE BIG FOOTBALL STAR
WELL, HE THROWS ME A PASS AND I CATCH IT
SO WE MEET FOR A DRINK AT THE BAR.

BOTH.

>AND WE DANCE
>AND I'M FLOATING ON CLOUD NINE

TED.

>THE RHYTHM IS MOVING MY FEET

MELINDA.

>MY HEART IS SKIPPING A BEAT

BOTH.

>AND WE DANCE
>AND I'M FLOATING ON CLOUD NINE
>I'M NOT THINKING WHAT'S RIGHT OR WHAT'S WRONG
>I HAVEN'T FELT THIS WAY IN SO LONG
>SO WE DANCE.

TED.

>I SENSE SHE IS WILLING AND ABLE,
>AS SHE FLASHES ME ONE SEXY SMILE
>IT IS LATE AND I'M REALLY NOT TIRED
>WHAT'S THE HARM IF WE TALK FOR A WHILE?

MELINDA.

>WE WERE BOYFRIEND AND GIRLFRIEND IN HIGH SCHOOL
>WE BROKE UP OVER SOME SILLY FIGHT
>NOW HE TELLS ME HE'S ALWAYS LOVED ME,
>WE MAKE PLANS TO MEET LATER THAT NIGHT.

BOTH.

>AND WE DANCE AND I'M FLOATING ON CLOUD NINE

TED.

>I DON'T CARE IF I'M MORALLY TWISTED

MELINDA.

>I FORGOT THAT THESE FEELINGS EXISTED

BOTH.

>AND WE DANCED AND I'M FLOATING ON CLOUD NINE

TED.

>I FEEL LIKE I DID AT SIXTEEN
>WHAT HAPPENS REMAINS TO BE SEEN

BOTH.

>AND WE DANCE

TED.

I'M WONDERING NOW WHAT SHE'D LOOK LIKE IN A BIKINI

MELINDA.

I'M WONDERING IF I SHOULD LET HIM BUY ME ANOTHER
MARTINI

(music break)

HE INVITES ME UPSTAIRS FOR A NIGHTCAP
I AM FLATTERED BUT CAUGHT UNAWARE

TED.

SHE SUGGESTS WE CONTINUE IN PRIVATE
AND BY PRIVATE, SHE MEANS GO UPSTAIRS

MELINDA.

THEN I THINK OF MY HUSBAND AND GOOD TIMES

TED.

AND MY WIFE AND THE YEARS WE'VE BEEN THROUGH

MELINDA.

AND IT'S THEN WHEN IT SUDDENLY HITS ME

TED.

AND I KNOW THEN AND THERE WHAT TO DO

*(The **GUY** and the **GAL** exit.)*

BOTH.

THEN WE DANCE AND I'M FLOATING ON CLOUD NINE

TED.

II FEELS GREAT TO BE BACK IN HER ARMS

MELINDA.

I'M REMINDED AGAIN OF HIS CHARMS

BOTH.

THEN WE DANCE AND I'M FLOATING ON CLOUD NINE

TED.

NEXT SHE NESTLES HER HEAD ON MY SHOULDER
IT FEELS SO GOOD JUST TO HOLD HER

BOTH.

OH THE THINGS THAT YOU LEARN WHEN YOU'RE OLDER –
AND WE DANCE!...

Scene Nineteen: AARP

(FRAMED BACKGROUND PHOTO – Living Room.
MAN ONE (RALPH) *enters looking at his mail.)*

RALPH. Junk.

Junk.

Bill.

(He sits down and continues to open his mail.)

Happy 50th. Cherish the past. Embrace the present. Welcome the future. Love, Sis. Nice.

Junk.

Bill.

What the…?

(A GREEK CHORUS: **MAN TWO, WOMAN ONE,** *and* **WOMAN TWO** *enter separately and each stand right behind* **RALPH** *singing the content of the letter as he reads. They are dressed in white robes with fig leaf head-dresses.)*

SONG: (16) "AARP"

CHORUS.

(MAN ONE enters.)

A.A.

(WOMAN TWO enters.)

R.

(WOMAN ONE enters.)

P.

ALL.

AARP! AARP! AARP!

RALPH. Oh, Shit!!!

CHORUS.

ANYONE FIFTY OR OVER CAN
GET THE GREAT BENEFITS
OF MEMBERSHIP IN AARP
FOR ONLY SIXTEEN DOLLARS A YEAR.

WOMAN ONE.

AND MEMBERSHIP INCLUDES
YOUR SPOUSE OR PARTNER – FREE!

MAN TWO.

ACCESS TO HEALTH INSURANCE,
AUTOMOBILE INSURANCE,
HOME OWNERS INSURANCE!

(**RALPH** *stops reading and puts the letter on the table.* **CHORUS** *immediately stops singing and they hold their breath while* **RALPH** *picks up another letter.* **RALPH** *goes back to AARP letter and chorus sings again.*)

WOMEN ONE & TWO.

GREAT DISCOUNTS ON TRAVEL
ONLINE SERVICES PHONE
AND MUCH MORE!

(**RALPH** *gets up from chair and begins to pace across the stage as he reads. The* **CHORUS** *follows.*)

CHORUS.

LEARN MORE ABOUT HEALTHY LIVING

(**RALPH** *closes letter* – **CHORUS** *stop. He opens letter* **CHORUS** *sing.*)

FINANCIAL

(**RALPH** *stops reading and* **CHORUS** *stops singing.*)

CHORUS.

PLANNING, AND
CONSUMER PROTECTION,
AND CARING FOR PARENTS
LOCAL CHAPTERS, DRIVING SAFETY COURSES,
AND A NATIONWIDE VOLUNTEER NETWORK

(**RALPH** *holds his ears shut* – *music gets muffled* – *when he takes his hands off his ears the music return, to normal.*)

AARP IS DEDICATED TO
ENHANCING THE QUALITY OF LIFE AS WE AGE.
ADDRESSING THE NEEDS AND CONCERNS
OF THE OVER FIFTY POPULATION

MAN TWO.

> INCLUDING THE SEVENTY-SIX MILLION STRONG
> EMPTY NEST GENERATION

CHORUS.

> GENERATION

WOMAN TWO.

> AND CHECK OUT OUR
> SPANISH-LANGUAGE NEWSPAPER

ALL.

> "SEGUNDA JUVENTUD."

Scene Twenty: He's Got To Eat

(FRAMED BACKGROUND PHOTO: APARTMENT BUILDING HALLWAY. **WOMAN TWO (LIZ)** *enters holding a casserole. A choreographed number.)*

SONG: (14) "CASSEROLE STROLL"

LIZ (WOMAN TWO). *(looking around)* Let's see...where is apartment 6D.

(sings)

POOR JACK I HEARD HIS WIFE IS GONE
AND I KNOW YOU CAN'T WAIT TOO LONG
IT'S A WELL KNOWN FACT IT'S A JUNGLE OUT THERE
AND A JUNGLE CALLS FOR JUNGLE WARFARE

(She does a sexy walking dance.)

SO, I'M, PLAYING THE CASSEROLE,
PLAYING THE CASSEROLE,
PLAYING THE CASSEROLE ROLE.
AND I'M DOIN' THE CASSEROLE,
DOIN' THE CASSEROLE,
DOIN' THE CASSEROLE STROLL.

*(**LIZ** turns to exit and **PEGGY** catches her. She is carrying a casserole in front, and concealing a bottle of gin behind her back.)*

PEGGY (WOMAN ONE). Oh, Liz. How are you? What are you doing here?

LIZ. *(surprised)* Well...Jack...um, and I...I thought...he'd be...well, he'd be lonely. And you? What do you have there, Peggy?

PEGGY.

I'VE KNOWN JACK FROM MANY A YEAR AGO
OUR FAMILIES ARE JUST LIKE KIN.
I'VE BROUGHT FOR HIM HIS FAVORITE CASSEROLE.
PLUS A BOTTLE OF BEEFEATER GIN.

(reveals the bottle of gin)

LIZ. Gosh, it's been a long time since I last saw you. I'm sorry to hear about…well, um…I understand you're a widow.

PEGGY. Actually, I'm not sure I'm a widow but when you don't hear from your husband in fourteen months, there's no point in keeping the soup warm.

PEGGY.

SO I'M,
PLAYIN' THE CASSEROLE,
PLAYIN' THE CASSEROLE
PLAYIN' THE CASSEROLE ROLE

BOTH.

AND WE'RE DOIN' THE CASSEROLE,
DOIN' THE CASSEROLE,
DOIN' THE CASSEROLE STROLL.

BOTH. *(sweetly)*

WHEN WE HEAR THERE'S A MAN ALL ALONE
WE QUICKLY COME TO SPREAD OUR GOOD CHEER.
THROUGH RAIN AND SNOW
WE BRING OUR MEALS ON WHEELS

PEGGY.

WE'RE KIND

LIZ.

WE'RE GOOD

BOTH. *(with a sneer)*

AND SINCERE.

BOTH.

RA TA TA TAH TA TA
RA TA TA TAH TA TA
RA TA TA TAH TA TA TAH.
RA TA TA TAH TA TA
RA TA TA TAH TA TA
RA TA TA TAH TA TA TAH.

(**MAN TWO (SUZIE)** *enters with large breasts and der-riere, wearing a short skirt, blond wig, pink high heels, a faux Gucci purse and a casserole.*)

SUZIE (MAN TWO).

> I'VE GOT THE EDGE
> NOW I'M GONNA USE MY YOUTH
> I NEED A MAN WITH LOTS OF MONEY
> I'LL SHOW HIM HOW TO WAKE UP AND REALLY LIVE
> WHEN I BECOME
>
> *(in baritone)*
>
> HIS HONEY.
>
> *(sexy vamp)*
>
> SO I'M
> PLAYING THE CASSEROLE
> PLAYING THE CASSEROLE
> PLAYING THE CASSEROLE ROLE

LIZ AND PEGGY. *(trying to compete)*

> YES, WE'RE
> DOIN' THE CASSEROLE
> DOIN' THE CASSEROLE
> DOIN' THE CASSEROLE STROLL

SUZIE (MAN TWO). *(outdoing them once again)*

> YES I'M
> PLAYIN' THE CASSEROLE
> PLAYIN' THE CASSEROLE
> PLAYIN' THE CASSEROLE ROLE

ALL. *(once again, unsuccessfully trying to imitate Suzie's sexy vamp)*

> AND, WE'RE
> DOIN' THE CASSEROLE
> DOIN' THE CASSEROLE
> DOIN' THE CASSEROLE...

LIZ. Ah, let's just forget it! I can't compete with that.

PEGGY. You got that right!

> *(They exit.)*

SUZIE (MAN TWO). *(On music, **SUZIE** circles the stage, comes down center, lifts casserole lid, and says in a manly baritone:)* Wanna piece?

> *(He kicks up his heels and sings.)*

ROLE!

VOICE OVER: ANSWERING MACHINE (DAUGHTER). *(slightly frenetically)* Hi Mom. I can't thank you enough for changing your plans and sitting with little Ali. She's so excited you're coming. A few details you'll need to know: *(child whining in background)* Not now, Ali I'm talking to Grandma. Where was I – oh yes. Number One: Ali has a slight fever but I don't think it's anything – just keep an eye on the rash on her tummy. Number Two: *(child whining noise)* Please Ali I'm almost finished. Um...oh yes, I'm sorry for leaving the kitchen in such a mess. I was running late. I knew you'd understand. And number three: The plumber said he would try and be there by three o'clock. If you need a toilet my neighbor said you could use hers. She left the key and I put it on the front table in the foyer, though I noticed Jack threw some papers there so you might have to look around. *(child whining noise)* And lastly, Ali stop it! Yes, number three, remember Mom, no videos or candy for Ali. She adores when you read to her. You are the *best* Mother. Thank you *soooo* much. Bye.

(beep)

Scene Twenty-One: Marvin

(FRAMED PHOTO: Blank. **MARVIN** *enters barefoot and assumes the 'lotus position'. He lets out a meditative "Hummmm.")*

(reciting as mantra)

MARVIN. I read that daily meditation relieves stress. Hmmmm.

I read doing the daily crossword puzzle prevents Alzheimer's. Hmmmm.

I read that a glass of red wine each day is good for your heart. Hmmm.

(snaps out of trance)

Now *that* got my attention. The problem is I only like white wine. So, seeking clarification I called Dr Wattles. "No, no," he assured me. In my case, white is perfectly acceptable. I guess he realized that nothing reduces stress like a glass of Sauvignon Blanc. And I need relaxation more than ever after recently partaking in a survey on the Web that informed me my life expectancy is 95.2, but, my *healthy* life expectancy is only 83.9. *(Avoiding a panic attack, he takes several deep breath as though purging.)* In with the good, out with the bad. In with the good, out with the bad. Hmmmm. *(once again, getting worked up)* While twelve years of decline was bad news for me, it was an even bigger blow to my kids when I told them if they put me in a nursing home I'd give all my money to charity! *(assumes different yoga pose)* Hmmmmm –

(He grabs holds of his back.)

Oh my back!

(A nurse appears.)

NURSE. *(in Gregorian chant)* Right this way, Marvin. Hmmmm.

MARVIN. Gotta go see the doctor!

Scene Twenty-Two: Ball Game

(PHOTO: Little League Baseball Game. **WOMAN ONE (EMILY)** *and* **MAN ONE (MICHAEL)** *meet for the first time at a little-league baseball game for each of their grandsons. Ambient ballpark noise in the background. She is on a bleacher bench. He is standing near by. They are both enthusiastically rooting for their own grandson.)*

(The sound of a bat hitting a ball is heard.)

EMILY. Go Kevin! You can do it! Round that base!

MICHAEL. Come on, Matthew – get in front of the ball!

EMILY. YES!!!

MICHAEL. *(He turns to her.)* That was quite a hit.

EMILY. He's my grandson.

MICHAEL. Yes, I've gathered. Oh, that's my Matthew over there. Second baseman.

EMILY. Oh, if Matt's your grandson, then Robyn's your daughter.

MICHAEL. You know Robyn?

EMILY. Yes, she's good friends with my daughter.

MICHAEL. So, you're Ellen's mother!?

(He motions to sit down next to her on the bench and she indicates it's ok.)

EMILY. In the flesh.

(You hear a ball being hit and **EMILY** *jumps to her feet.)*

Kevin – stay on second! …Yes! Nice hit! Oh, I'm sorry you were saying?

MICHAEL. I was sorry to hear about your late husband. My daughter said he was quite a guy.

EMILY. Thank you. I understand you're a widower. Tough, isn't it?

MICHAEL. Yes, I never realized –

(We hear a ball being hit. **MICHAEL** *jumps to his feet.)*

Yes. Yes! Yes, at a boy, Matt. Way to go.

(He claps for his grandson.)

EMILY. It's especially hard when you've been happily married.

MICHAEL. No one understands unless they've been there.

EMILY. You can say that again.

MICHAEL. *(enthusiastically)* My Katie… *(He pauses, catching himself from getting emotional.)* took charge of everything. *(with levity)* Now if I want to go out, I not only have to make the plans, but worse yet, I have to decide what to wear.

EMILY. *(laughing)* I used to pick out all of Roger's clothes, too.

EMILY. So what kind of things do you like to do?

MICHAEL. Well, I like to eat and travel. Not much fun alone. So what keeps you busy?

EMILY. Well, I'm interested in politics. I never miss Sunday morning's FACE THE NATION. My kids tease me I'm perfectly capable to advise President Obama if he ever decides to call.

MICHAEL. And when you're not advising?

EMILY. *(A moment. She's a little taken aback.)* I…um…I like going to the theater. Musicals in particular.

MICHAEL. I like musicals, too! When they're as good as 'Guys and Dolls.'

EMILY. Oh, I love that one. I played Adelaide in high school.

MICHAEL. Get out of here! I played Nathan Detroit in my school!

EMILY. Oh, what a coincidence.

MICHAEL. So sue me. *(They enjoy a good laugh. A beat.)* You know you're very easy to talk to.

EMILY. Well, thank you. You too. It's so nice talking to someone…like, you know, face to face.

MICHAEL. Really? As opposed to what?

EMILY. Oh nothing.

(A ball is hit. She jumps to her feet.)

EMILY. Oh Kevin! Go! Go for home! Go, go, go! *(He's tagged out.)* Oh darn.

MICHAEL. Yes, yes! Good one, Matt!

(He turns to EMILY, slightly embarrassed by his excitement over his grandson's achievement.)

Aw, nice try! Well, it was a good game. Say uh, are you taking Kevin for ice cream?

EMILY. As a matter of fact, I am.

MICHAEL. Would you like to come with us?

EMILY. *(pause)* Well, I guess the kids would like that.

MICHAEL. By the way, I'm Michael. Michael Stockman.

EMILY. Emily Anderson. It's nice to meet you.

MICHAEL. Likewise.

(They come forward and speak to the audience, without acknowledging the other.)

EMILY. That night my daughter calls me to say Kevin told her we went for ice cream with Michael.

MICHAEL. My phone's ringing off the hook when I walk in the door. Naturally, it's my daughter. She's thrilled. She heard we had ice cream together. I told Matt to keep it between us! KIDS! The next morning I call Emily to offer her a ride to the game on Thursday. I don't want to call too early, so I wait until 8 o'clock.

EMILY. 7:46.

MICHAEL. I've been a widower for a year and a half and have had my share of dates but somehow, she's different. She's so full of life!

EMILY. He has a great sense of humor.

MICHAEL. I look forward to driving her to the games.

EMILY. This goes on through the playoffs.

MICHAEL. I never made a pass at her.

EMILY. He's a perfect gentleman.

MICHAEL. If I did my daughter would kill me.

EMILY. Then one night he invites me to the opera.

MICHAEL. I know she likes opera.

EMILY. He knows I like opera. I get all dressed up. It feels good. I put on high heels.

MICHAEL. I take her to Bistro 33.

EMILY. Our tickets are fifth row center.

MICHAEL. The lights dim…

EMILY. The conductor lifts his baton. The overture begins… the curtain slowly rises –

MICHAEL. The set is spectacular.

EMILY. It takes my breath away and in my enthusiasm my hand just – just reaches for his hand..

(They take hold of each other's hand, still without looking at each other.)

…and I can't believe what's happening…it's like, in the movies! After all we're not kids, and it's not supposed to happen twice in a lifetime, but my heart is, actually pounding. I feel like a giddy teenager. I look at him. The smile on his face-

MICHAEL. *(interrupts)* From that day on, we've been each other's…

BOTH. "Significant other."

MICHAEL. …One day after about ten months, my daughter calls to say, "Hi, Dad, listen…all of Emily's kids, and all of ours have decided to take a vacation together. We talked and we all want you and Emily to join us."

EMILY. So my daughter calls to ask where we're planning to *sleep* on the trip. I'm… I'm caught off guard. And *that's* when she reminds me: *she* has children. The lessons I taught her are coming back to haunt me!

*(Now, **EMILY** sits back down on the bench and turns to speak to **MICHAEL**.)*

I'm soooo embarrassed!

MICHAEL. Don't let it bother you.

EMILY. I'm confused.

MICHAEL. We're adults.

EMILY. I'm upset.

(He gets down on his knee and looks into her eyes.)

MICHAEL. We're engaged.

(pause)

EMILY. *(coyly)* We're engaged? *(long pause)* Cool!

MICHAEL. *(a little nervous but excited)* Let's…go get a bite. We've got lots to talk about.

(PHOTO: Upscale restaurant. **EMILY** *and* **MICHAEL** *change to appropriate dining attire.* **MAN TWO** *enters as a waiter.* **MICHAEL** *holds the chair for* **EMILY** *and they are seated at a beautifully set table)*

SONG: (18) "NEW FIRSTS" REPRISE

*(***WAITER*** *hands them wine list.* **MICHAEL** *makes a selection.)*

EMILY.

SO MANY NEW FIRSTS
WHEN YOU'RE A NEW PAIR

MICHAEL.

SO MANY NEW FIRSTS
WE NOW GET TO SHARE

*(***WAITER*** *lights candles.)*

EMILY.

FIRST CANDLELIGHT DINNER –WE SIT AND DISCUSS

MICHAEL.

AND ALL THE WHILE KNOWING
THAT SOMETHING IS GROWING,

EMILY.

SOMETHING IN US

BOTH.

SO MANY FIRSTS
WE'LL FACE EACH DAY.

*(***WAITER*** *gives them menus.)*

EMILY.

LIKE LEARNING YOUR NEEDS –

MICHAEL.

LEARNING WHAT NOT TO SAY!

FIRST CONCERT TOGETHER.

EMILY.

FIRST TIME WE'LL SKI

FIRST SCRAPBOOK WE'LL START

OF JUST YOU AND ME

BUT I'LL ALWAYS LOVE ROGER

MICHAEL.

AND I'LL ALWAYS LOVE KATE

EMILY.

WE ARE WHO WE ARE NOW BECAUSE OF OUR MATE

BOTH.

BUT WHILE I'M STILL HERE I NEED TO GO ON

THE FUTURE LOOKS BRIGHT

'CAUSE AFTER TONIGHT

TOMORROW WILL DAWN.

(WAITER pours wine.)

EMILY.

I USED TO THINK

I COULD LIVE WITHOUT LOVE.

BUT LATELY IT'S JUST ABOUT ALL I THINK OF.

MICHAEL.

I USED TO THINK

LIFE WAS SOMETHING I HAD.

BOTH.

WHO WOULD HAVE DREAMED –

THERE'D BE MORE WE COULD ADD.

TWO BROKEN HEARTS NOW

TOGETHER ARE WHOLE.

(WAITER appears.)

MICHAEL.

THE WAITER IS WAITING DEAR

EMILY. *(EMILY thinks a minute and replies)* I'll have…Dover Sole.

(They kiss.)

Scene Twenty-Three: Finale

(PHOTO: "THE KIDS LEFT. THE DOG DIED. NOW WHAT?" LOGO)

SONG: (19) " NOW WHAT?" REPRISE

*(***WOMAN ONE*** enters.)*

WOMAN ONE.
TIME MOVES ON AND IT LEAVES YOU INSECURE
'CAUSE WITH NO GUARANTEES YOU FIND
NOTHING IS FOR SURE

*(***MAN TWO*** enters.)*

MAN TWO.
THINGS ARE FINE
THEN YOU'RE FORCED TO MAKE A CHANGE

BOTH.
AND EVERYTHING NEW SEEEMS SO TERRIBLY STRANGE

*(***MAN ONE & WOMAN ONE*** join in.)*

ALL.
THE HOUSE IS EMPTY

WOMAN TWO. *(speaks)* The kitchen stove broke and I'm not fixing it.

ALL.
THE KIDS ARE GONE

MAN ONE. *(speaks)* Now, I get to enjoy my wife!

ALL.
THE DOG IS BURIED

MAN TWO. *(speaks)* Goodbye pooper-scooper!

ALL.
WE'RE MOVIN' ON!

WOMAN TWO. *(speaks)* I've always wanted to explore Indonesia.

MAN TWO. *(speaks)* How bout exploring Florida?

ALL.
WE'VE LEARNED GREAT LESSONS

WOMAN ONE. *(speaks)* I'm learning Taichi!

MAN ONE. *(speaks)* I'm studying Buddhism!

WOMAN TWO. *(speaks)* I'm studying fencing.

ALL.

TO BUILD UPON

WOMAN ONE. *(speaks)* It's not how you begin the act – it's how you leave the stage!

ALL.

AND THE WORLD IS SUDDENLY BIGGER
AND THE TIMES ARE SIZZLING HOT

WE'VE GOT DREAMS AND CAUSES AND PASSIONS
AND THE WILL TO GIVE 'EM A SHOT

'CAUSE THE TIME IS OURS FOR THE TAKING
IF WE TAKE THE TIME THAT WE'VE GOT

(answering machine)

(beep)

OFF STAGE ANSWERING MACHINE.

DAUGHTER. Hey, Mom & Dad. Good news! I'm moving back home!

ALL.

NOW WHAT?

The End

PROJECTIONS

Photos to be projected on framed backdrop appropriate to setting of scene.

PROPERTIES

2 chairs – Scene 2
1 16" parsons tables – Scene two
1 24" diameter x 29"h round table (two table cloths) – Scenes 4 & 21
2 computer tables, approximately 29"h X 18"w X 36" – Scenes 6, 10 & 16
1 podium for top on computer table – Scene 6
1 free standing full length mirror (no glass) – Scene 4
1 coat stand – Scene 4
1 rolling clothing rack with hanging "designer" clothes – Scene 7
1 bench for store – Scene 7
1 bleacher/bench – Scene 21

1 wine glass and wine bottle – Scene 6
1 bottle of Beefeaters gin – Scene 20

1 Weber Grill – Scene 8
2 grocery hand baskets, with groceries – Scene 17
2 (non working) lap top computers – Scenes 10 & 16.
3 casseroles dishes – Scene 20
1 land phone – Scene 2
1 cell phone – Scene 2.
1 laundry basket full of toys – Scene 5
1 blow-up mattress – Scene 5
Several board games – Scene 5
2 Forks, 2 Plates, and wedding cake – Scene 12
3 togas and fig leaf headdresses – Scene 19

SPECIAL COSTUMES

In addition to normal attire, appropriate to each scene, listed here are suggested "specialty" costumes.
3 white lab coats – Scene 3
1 hospital gown – Scene 3
1 grilling apron, with baseball hat – Scene 11
1 oversized dress with phony bust, derriere, and high heels – Scene 20

OTHER TITLES AVAILABLE FROM SAMUEL FRENCH

FLAMINGO COURT

Luigi Creatore

Comedy / 3m, 2f, with doubling (Character ages range from 60s to 89. 5 to 10 actors may be used depending on doubling or tripling roles.)

This three part "slice of life" takes place in three different condos and has audiences laughing at the truth they see in what might be their own neighbors - only zanier. *Flamingo Court* has ten characters. In the New York production, five actors played all the roles. Producers may want to follow the above pattern, or cast up to ten actors. In any case, audiences respond to this trilogy with uproarious laughter and leave feeling they have experienced great entertainment.

ANGELINA, in 104, is a Neil-Simonesque three character piece that starts with smiles and grows into a hilarious, audience-howling ending.

CLARA, in 204, is the shortest (ten to twelve minutes) piece. It deals with two characters in a poignant look at the problems of aging and separation. Powerful theater!

HARRY, in 304, a five character play - and the wackiest - deals with an eighty-nine year-old gentleman who is battling his greedy daughter at the same time that he gets involved with an aging hooker. When the daughter and the hooker meet "the audience laughs up a Florida-worthy hurricane!" (John Simon, *Bloomberg News*)

"Laughs galore! Without question, the funniest play in New York today! A 'must-see' theatrical event for audiences of all ages. Power-house performances from Anita Gillette and Jamie Farr."
– UPI

SAMUELFRENCH.COM